PHILADELPHIA

"I can't think of a more immediate, more challenging, and absolutely gripping story for these times in America than the one told by the very fine novelist Christopher Davis within the pages of *Philadelphia*."

— JONATHAN DEMME

Also by Christopher Davis

JOSEPH AND THE OLD MAN
VALLEY OF THE SHADOW
THE BOYS IN THE BARS

PHILADELPHIA

A Novel by
Christopher Davis

Based on
the Screenplay Written by
Ron Nyswaner

BANTAM BOOKS
New York   Toronto   London   Sydney   Auckland

PHILADELPHIA

A Bantam Book
Bantam hardcover edition / January 1994
Bantam paperback edition / August 1994

0-553-56913-9

Published simultaneously in the United States and Canada

Bantam Books are published by Bantam Books, a division of Bantam
Doubleday Dell Publishing Group, Inc. Its trademark, consisting of
the words "Bantam Books" and the portrayal of a rooster, is Registered
in U.S. Patent and Trademark Office and in other countries. Marca
Registrada. Bantam Books, 1540 Broadway, New York, New York
10036.

PRINTED IN THE UNITED STATES OF AMERICA

OPM   0 9 8 7 6 5 4 3 2 1

ACKNOWLEDGMENTS

Someday I may write a book about writing a novel from a film, but until then there are many people I should thank: Esther Margolis, who, as I wrote in this book about a character, was just the right combination of drill sergeant and mother; Rob Weisbach, who was always enthusiastic and who made me think; Neda Armian at Clinica Estetico, who was unflaggingly kind and helpful, and Valerie Thomas, whose mixture of restraint and good judgment was invaluable to the process; Barbara Lakin at TriStar Pictures, who immediately acceded to my every request; Steven Sayre and Keith MacGregor from my office, who were more than understanding even when I showed up for a staggering four or five hours a week, and also from my office, Georges Rios, who, although overworked himself, took on some of my work as well, and Bill Byler, who was always there to listen; Kathy Silva for her careful eye; Ron Nyswaner for his moving screenplay; Edward Hibbert and Neil Olson, from Donadio and Ashworth, who put this all together; and Jonathan Demme, who truly believes in his work.

More than anyone, however, I must thank my best friend, my severest critic, and my lover, Hank Irwin.

Christopher Davis
New York
August 1993

One

Jamey Collins, a junior associate at the old-line Phila-delphia law firm of Wyant, Wheeler, Hellerman, Tet-low, and Brown, was late, but then he had been late for almost everything from the time he was a child. In his early thirties, balding, nondescript, the kind of person one forgets meeting within a few hours, he was too old to be a junior associate, but he had started law school late. It had taken him through most of his twenties to decide what he wanted to do with his life, and even then, law school was almost an accident. He was, to put it succinctly, a chronic procrastinator: If papers were due at 5:00 he would reluc-tantly turn his attention to them sometime around 3:30.

This time, because Jamey was late, his boss on the case, senior associate Andrew Beckett, was in front of Judge Eu-nice Tate without the report he needed, arguing against a motion for a TRO brought by some low-life ambulance chaser named Joe Miller who specialized in personal injury lawsuits. Around the firm Judge Tate was referred to as "very tough," and sometimes, after an attorney from the firm had emerged scathed from a session in her courtroom, as "that bitch on wheels in a black robe."

Jamey charged up the front steps of Philadelphia's City Hall — solid, massive, but ornate: a temple to the preeminence of Government. Cursing under his breath, scattering people before him. He ran down the hall, decided against the elevator, and ran two steps at a time up the main staircase — well-polished Italian marble worn in the center. When he finally reached the outer room in Judge Tate's chambers, he stopped to catch his breath, but the clerks and attorneys working at the library table there barely looked up. Jamey knew he was in trouble because he could already hear the attorneys inside arguing.

"This construction site imposes a grave and irreversible danger to an unsuspecting public!"

That must be the ambulance chaser, Jamey thought. Boy, what a sleazebag.

"Your Honor," Andrew Beckett said, not waiting for Joe Miller to finish, "there has not been one shred of evidence, not one, linking any of the plaintiff's symptoms with my client's new development project."

Jamey pushed open the door without knocking and without thinking about the possible consequences of Judge Tate's wrath. The judge, however, calmly seated at her desk and slightly bemused by the attorneys arguing in front of her, ignored Jamey.

"That's not true!" Miller said.

"Then let's see it!" Andrew challenged him.

"One at a time, please," Judge Tate said. "Mr. Miller?"

"You're late," Andrew whispered to Jamey, and Jamey apologized. This was the first time Jamey had been in a judge's chambers and he was surprised to see that it was just an ordinary-looking law office with obligatory floor-to-ceiling wooden bookcases filled with case reporters, not nearly as impressive as some of the offices back at Wyant, Wheeler. Somehow, he had expected more; perhaps a gavel on the desk. He also thought that Judge Tate, thin, middle-aged with graying hair, did not look all that ferocious. Underestimating people was another of Jamey's weaknesses.

Joe Miller glared at Andrew and Jamey for a moment, wondering what was in the envelope Jamey was carrying and why it was so important, and then he turned his attention back to Judge Tate. "Your Honor, since Kendell Corporation began construction, my client's neighborhood has been enshrouded in a cloud of foul-smelling, germ-carrying, pestilent dust! My client—"

"Your Honor!" Andrew tried to interrupt.

"One at a time!" Judge Tate said. "Mr. Miller, I assume you were not finished."

Joe missed, or ignored, the sarcasm in her voice. "No, Your Honor, I was not," he said. "As I was saying, because of this foul cloud caused by Kendell Corporation's disregard of basic human rights, my client is being forced to breathe known carcinogens daily. Not only is my client outraged—

not only am *I* outraged—but the other residents in the neighborhood are outraged. They're coming forth on a daily basis to join this action, this action for justice!"

"Your Honor," Andrew said, "I submit there were no additional complaints until"—he took a breath, looked at Joe, and looked back at the judge—*"Counselor* began knocking on doors to drum up a little business."

"That's an outrageous and unprofessional accusation," Joe said.

Jamey smiled and the judge caught him.

"Gentlemen!" Judge Tate was beginning to get a headache, and she had had enough of this pointless motion.

"Sorry, Your Honor," Andrew said. "May I continue?"

Judge Tate nodded.

"This 'pestilent dust,' as *Counselor* calls it, has appeared on only three occasions. Only three. Each time samples have been examined by an independent laboratory, and we have the results."

Jamey handed Andrew a document and a small plastic bag from behind, and Andrew scanned the document quickly, although he already knew what it contained. Then he said solemnly, "It's limestone, Your Honor. Limestone. Messy but innocuous." Andrew examined the bag.

"May I see that, please," Judge Tate asked.

"Certainly, Your Honor."

Andrew handed her the document and pointed out the summary of conclusions.

"Innocuous!" Joe said.

"Defined by *Webster's* as harmless," Andrew told him. He handed Joe the bag of limestone dust and then turned and nodded a dismissal at Jamey, who would have liked to see how the judge decided but understood Andrew's order.

"I know what it means," Joe said. He stopped to think for a few seconds. Nobody noticed when Jamey left and closed the door. "Your Honor, nobody is thinking about the *children* here. Imagine how the children in the neighborhood have been made to feel."

Andrew rolled his eyes, but the judge pretended not to notice. She was well aware of the difference in power and status of the two law firms represented before her, and she was determined to be as fair as possible.

"Imagine the pounding of construction always ringing in the children's ears as this skyscraper, a tribute to mankind's greed, grows daily, casting an ominous shadow over their lives, filling them with dread even as they are surrounded with a black, toxic fog, blocking out the sun while poisoning their lungs! And Counselor calls it harmless! Remember the children!"

A little part of Andrew watched the proceedings from a distance, and he thought about how lucky he was to be part of a great firm like Wyant, Wheeler, instead of a personal injury firm like Joe's. Personal injury law is usually perceived by lawyers as being the bottom of the profession; its practitioners are often thought of as lower than practitioners of corporate law. Andrew thought that personal injury law was a little like blackmail: Sue for a large sum of money in hopes that the defendant will be intimidated into settling for some smaller sum. It was a fact, Andrew knew, that most personal injury cases never come to trial but are settled for much less than the original demand, and he wondered how often Joe Miller actually came to trial. Although Andrew had little respect for the kind of law Joe practiced, there was something about Joe personally that he did respect; Joe was aggressive but never loud, and he reacted very quickly to each challenge.

"I assume you have something to add," Judge Tate said to Andrew, and he snapped back to reality; his job was to win.

"Your Honor," Andrew said, "Counselor is attempting to portray my client as some hideous manifestation of depravity and corruption. Nothing could be further from the truth." Andrew stopped and looked directly at Joe. "Counselor knows that Kendell Construction *builds* neighborhoods. It does not destroy them."

Andrew had had Judge Tate's sympathy until then, but Kendell had a terrible reputation and was always in court for something, and when the judge started to smile, Andrew knew that he was losing her, and Joe knew it too.

"Your Honor," Joe said, "Kendell builds buildings— for profit, may I add—Kendell does not build neighborhoods."

But you missed the important argument, Andrew thought. "Your Honor," he said, "granting a restraining order on this construction site will throw seven hundred and fifty-three Philadelphians out of work. In addition, it will lend validation to this contemptible and groundless nuisance suit, which has not only taken advantage of this court's patience, but is an example of the rapacious litigation that today is threatening the very fabric of our society!"

Judge Tate looked at them both, and when Joe opened his mouth to answer she held up her hand. "Let's not go off the deep end here," she said. "I thought we were just talking about some dust."

"Toxic dust!" Joe corrected.

"Limestone!" Andrew answered.

"I am not finished," Judge Tate said. "Mr. Miller, you've made an articulate and compelling presentation, but I don't believe you've proven irreparable harm."

"Not yet, Your Honor," Joe said.

"Request for a temporary restraining order denied," Judge Tate said.

"Your Honor—" Joe began again.

"Denied!" Judge Tate stood and motioned them toward the door.

Joe Miller was not pleased. He made his living on personal injury cases, yet he did not receive a dime, not even for expenses, unless he won. Of course, if he did win, he kept up to 30 percent of the award, and sometimes even more, although he always had to be mindful of the Bar's canon of ethics when setting percentages. Attorneys had gotten rich practicing personal injury law, but not Joe: So far, he had not hit the big one. What he needed was a nice hundred-million-dollar medical malpractice case.

As he walked to the elevator, he looked at Andrew, the yes man from Wyant, Wheeler in the expensive suit. Joe knew he never could have gone that route, not because he wasn't a good enough lawyer—in fact, he was very good, particularly on the fine points of civil procedure, and he was, as lawyers say, quick on his feet—but because he never could have survived the seven years of hazing that associates in large firms undergo in the hope of making partner. Even then, only a very few made it. Give a firm seven years of blood with a good chance of being told at the end, sorry, you didn't make it, you're out: That was not for Joe. Plus, and this was a very big plus, he was black and there were very few black partners at major law firms, a situation that Joe did not think was going to change in the near future.

Joe and Andrew walked together in silence, then waited, side by side, at the elevator bank. The elevator finally came and Andrew and Joe stood aside to let a man on crutches get on first. Then Joe motioned to Andrew, after you, and Andrew did the same to Joe. There was a slight stand-off, neither of them speaking, but then the doors started to close and they crowded in together. The man on crutches hit the button with the tip of a crutch, and Andrew immediately took up a position in a back corner, pulled out a small tape recorder, and began dictating part of a brief for a different case. Doesn't he think he's important, Joe thought, so he took out his own recorder and did the same. Although they both pretended to ignore each other, they both were listening, each thinking that the other was pretty good, although neither ever would have admitted it. The man on crutches thought they both were slightly crazy.

The dictating was interrupted by the annoying beep of a cellular phone, and both Joe and Andrew took out their phones at exactly the same time. In different circumstances, they probably would have laughed, or at least smiled a little, but this time Andrew just pointed to Joe's phone and said, "You," then put his phone away and resumed dictating. Joe, of course, tried to make his call, which was actually his secretary relaying a message from his wife about dinner, sound much more important.

Iris did not understand why Joe wasn't responding to her questions. "Why aren't you talking to me?" she demanded.

"Right," Joe said.

"Right what?"

"That's right," Joe said.

"Do you want to tell me what is going on?" Iris said, as the elevator reached the ground floor and the doors opened.

"Got to go," Joe said, and he pushed the button and disconnected her.

Andrew was in a hurry. He was out the door as soon as it opened. "Client of yours?" he said to Joe, nodding at the man on crutches as he left.

"Funny," Joe said, "very funny." He let the man pass and watched as Andrew hurried away. "Asshole," he said under his breath. Joe watched the man on crutches for another moment, and then ran after him. "Yo! Sir!"

The man stopped and waited.

"If there's anything I can do for you, give me a call," Joe said. He put a business card into the man's pocket and hurried on. The man waited until Joe was out of sight then took out the card and tore it into pieces and threw them on the floor.

———

Outside, after he made a quick call to his office to report on the outcome of the motion, Andrew was looking at his watch on one arm and impatiently waving down a cab with the other; he was due at his doctor's office now, and he had to be back at his firm in a couple of hours. After he gave the driver the address, he immediately opened his briefcase and started reading background for his next assignment, and before he was aware of time passing he was at his destination.

Dr. Gillman's office was on a quiet residential street lined with brownstones, where trees rustled in the breeze and sparrows sang from windowsills. As an internist with a specialty in infectious diseases, a good part of Dr. Gillman's practice was treating AIDS. Andrew had found her because of the publicity surrounding a lawsuit brought by her neighbors and landlord several years earlier when her AIDS practice began to grow. The case was complicated and nasty: Essentially everyone wanted her out because her patients were posing a "mortal threat" to the community. Dr. Gillman had fought hard and won, and the case had gotten national publicity. A year later, the entire story was in the Philadelphia newspapers when her defending attorney died of AIDS himself. Andrew had followed the case in the press, and then when he had tested positive for HIV four years ago, he decided to call Dr. Gillman. It was a good match: As Miguel often told their friends, this doctor had just the right combination of drill sergeant and mother.

Dr. Gillman emphasized outpatient care whenever possible; "It's just good medicine," she'd say. "Who wants to be in a smelly building surrounded by strangers when you can be at home surrounded by people you know?" Her office was a confirmation of her beliefs: pleasant, calm, lighted clearly but softly, not with the harsh fluorescent lights common in doctors' offices, and it was filled with patients who received intravenous drugs or inhalation therapy there instead of at an outpatient clinic at a hospital. Andrew knew many of the patients from previous visits, and he said hello and smiled and waved to various people as he went to the desk to check in.

"It's my favorite lawyer," the receptionist said. Andrew was uncomfortable with that, and he looked around the room again quickly. There was no one who looked as though they would know anyone at Wyant, Wheeler, though, and no one seemed interested anyway.

"Yeah, and I've had a hard day chasing ambulances," Andrew said. "Sometime I'm going to catch one."

The receptionist laughed. "Whenever you're ready. You know the drill."

Andrew nodded—he did know the drill—and took an empty seat next to an IV pole as a nurse came into the room with a full IV bag.

"Hey guy, how're we doing today?" the nurse said.

"*I'm* doing fine, Tyrone, how about you?"

"Now don't you be correcting my English, sweetheart," Tyrone said as he examined Andrew's arm. "I can speak the Queen's English as well as you can when I want to, which isn't often.

"You know," he said, "you really should think about getting a catheter. It'd make things so much easier; I wouldn't have to stick you all the time."

This was a topic they had covered before. Not only did Andrew not like the idea of some permanent needle in his arm, or worse, in his chest, but it would be very difficult to conceal from people at the office. Andrew said nothing.

"Well, just think about it," Tyrone said. "Ready?" he asked.

Andrew nodded, and Tyrone worked quickly. God, Andrew hated those needles, and although he tried not to, he gasped as it went in.

"Sorry, guy," Tyrone said, but it was done, and after

he checked to make sure that the flow was correct, Tyrone patted Andrew's shoulder and left to get medicine for his next patient.

Andrew took a Walkman and some papers from his briefcase, but before he began to work he looked around the room and his mind started to wander. Like most of the patients there, Andrew had full-blown AIDS, as it is often called to distinguish it from merely being infected with the HIV virus. He had had pneumocystis carinii pneumonia almost a year ago and now he had KS plus some other less severe problems. Dr. Gillman had repeatedly asked him to slow down, had told him that stress was bad for him. But slowing down was not something that Andrew understood, and he thought that a life without some stress would be awfully boring and probably not worth living. He always billed at least sixty hours a week, which meant he was spending even more time than that at the office or working on office matters at home. Plus, he somehow always found time to spend with Miguel, his lover of eight years.

Andrew thought about Miguel for a moment. He decided it was time they had some fun. Perhaps a weekend in New York; take in the new show at the Metropolitan Museum, maybe, and then dinner someplace — Miguel loved a little restaurant in the East Village where the waitresses wore safety pins through their noses and the food was macrobiotic. Andrew's taste ran more to the elegant Four Seasons. Andrew enjoyed the rewards of his success, but he was always willing to compromise for Miguel.

Andrew looked around the room. This was the AIDS that was rarely seen in the press: no shrill demonstrations, no grim body counts, no hysterical accusations of murder, just a group of men and women fighting a disease and at the same time trying to maintain their normal lives as much as possible. For a few minutes Andrew just listened to the conversations around him. A healthy-looking woman, Susan, was talking to a not-so-healthy-looking man, Rick, about weight, a topic of major concern among all AIDS patients.

"So how much weight have you lost?" Susan asked.

"Fifty pounds!" Rick said. It did not seem to bother him as much as it should. His face was terribly gaunt, and he did not look as though there was much more weight he could lose. "Can you believe it? I'm disappearing. The other day my sons and I were in a restaurant and when I ordered coffee the waiter asked me if I wanted sugar or Sweet'n Low. I said, 'Do I look like I should be on a diet?' "

"My God!" Susan said, rolling her eyes. She still looked healthy and robust.

"Then my oldest boy says, 'Dad, when did you start losing all that weight?' "

"Does your son know you've got HIV?" Susan asked.

"Yeah, I told both my sons." Rick was silent for a moment, thinking fondly of his boys. "You know," he said, "their reaction was interesting. My oldest seemed really involved intellectually, you know, trying to understand the disease and all, but my youngest didn't want to deal with it. But they're both really great, real champs, you know."

Like Miguel, Andrew thought.

"That's great," Susan said, "you have family to support you."

"It makes a big difference," Rick said, "particularly now that my eyes are going on me." He laughed. "I actually got hit in the head with a football the other day because I couldn't see it. Me! The strange thing is that they're starting to become part of the cure. They say stuff like 'Dad, did you remember to take your medicine?' and it makes them feel they have some kind of responsibility in making me well."

That's not so strange, Andrew thought, and he thought about how supportive his own family had been — his parents, his two brothers, his sister.

"That's great," Susan said. "I don't have family, so I have to depend on friends and support groups. You're very lucky."

"You have family too," Rick said. "Family are really just people who care, people who are there for you."

Indeed, Andrew thought, and he turned on his Walkman and listened to the music. He sometimes said that classical music kept him sane, and it may not have been totally inaccurate. When he was tired or under pressure, he could let himself go, let himself flow with the music, and when it was over he always felt better, refreshed. He particularly liked to listen to music when he was receiving treatments. It helped him forget what was running into his arm; it helped him forget the nasty little virus that was biding its time inside him; it helped him forget the lesions that were growing on his body, slowly but ever so surely consuming it. That day, however, it was difficult to forget the lesions, because not only had he found one on his forehead that morning but also sitting near him was a young man whose face was covered with them. I hope I die before I ever look like that, Andrew thought. The appearance of the young man made Andrew so uncomfortable he had to close his eyes, and he concentrated on the music for a few minutes and then bent down and picked up a brief and began working. He did not look at the young man again.

"Andy."

Andrew was lost in the music and in his work and did not hear.

"Andy!"

"Oh hi, Doc," he said. "Sorry, I was kind of out of it there."

"Your blood work came back this morning," Dr. Gillman said. "I'll be back in a few minutes to discuss it with you."

"I'll be here," Andrew said.

It took almost two hours for the IV to be finished, and by then Andrew only had thirty minutes to get back to his office for a conference call that had been scheduled more than a week earlier for that time, so as usual, Andrew was in a hurry, and also as usual, Andrew used every available minute for work: As soon as he gave the cabdriver his destination he started looking at documents and did not look up again until they stopped in front of the Wheeler building. Andrew did not wait for the driver to make change, which resulted in a tip that was much too large (and a very happy driver), and he rushed into the building, stopping an elevator with his hand just as the doors were about to close. He stepped out on his floor exactly three minutes before the conference call was scheduled to begin.

The social structure of a large U.S. law firm is simple: It is entirely feudal. At the very bottom are the members of the support staff—the non-attorneys, the serfs. To them, everyone else is Mr. or Ms., and an attorney's least wish is their command. Slightly above the staff are the paralegals. They generally have small offices with no windows, and they do not have secretaries; they do most of the drudge work in the firm. Above the paralegals are the junior associates: Junior associates rarely address partners by their first names; in fact, junior associates do not even know most of the partners. Associates just out of law school know less about the law than the paralegals, however the gulf in status between the two groups is unbridgeable: Associates are *attorneys*, and even the newest one has more authority than the most experienced paralegal.

When associates first arrive they generally share offices and secretaries, but as they become more and more senior, their status and the accompanying perquisites grow—they have their own secretaries, they occupy nice offices, they work more closely with partners, and they have junior associates working for them. Occasionally an associate becomes a real star, someone whom everyone assumes will be made a partner in the firm, someone who gets the best cases, someone who works closely with the best-known partners, but these are rare.

There is another kind of associate, too: the drone. Everyone, except possibly the associate, knows that this employee has virtually no chance of being made a member of the firm. He is just there to perform tasks that, however routine, must be performed by attorneys, and at the end of seven or eight years his affiliation with the firm is ended with a handshake and perhaps a couple of months' severance.

And above everyone are the lords, otherwise known as the partners. The partners have huge offices, battalions of secretaries, their own dining room, their own bathrooms. Partners socialize with associates, but only infrequently; they almost never socialize with paralegals or support staff, except for the occasional partner who divorces his wife and marries his secretary, a practice that is frowned upon but tolerated.

Andrew was *the* star associate at Wyant, Wheeler. It was evident by the way that two of the firm's senior partners, Kenneth Killcoyne and Robert Seidman, greeted Andrew as he rushed out of the elevator and down the hall toward his office.

"That was solid work on the Kendell situation, Andy," Mr. Killcoyne called.

"Top-notch, Mr. Beckett," said Mr. Seidman, the youngest of the firm's four senior partners and the only one whose hair was not totally gray. The "Mr. Beckett" was said with respect and friendship, and Andrew smiled. "Charles will be pleased," Mr. Seidman added. By "Charles," he meant Charles Wheeler, who was one of the name partners of the firm, roughly equivalent to God in the feudal analogy. Andrew was indeed a star, and since he knew it he did not take the time to stop and chat. "Thanks," he said as he rushed on, "I've got a conference call."

"Anthea," he said, when he finally saw someone he wanted to talk with. "You're just the paralegal extraordinaire I wanted to see. Walk with me."

Anthea laughed. "I know what that means," she said, "and the answer is no. I can't work late tonight."

Andrew gave her his best smile and said, "We're talking about a nice dinner later."

"And that won't work either," she said. "I can't work late because I have a class. Go exploit someone else. And by the way, since you've asked —"

"Your exam!" Andrew interrupted.

"Thank you," Anthea said. "Ninety-eight. And now I've got to go."

"Ninety-*eight*? Ninety-eight! Congratulations, Counselor. You're going to be the most successful lawyer who ever went to law school at night!"

Andrew reached the secretary's station and his secretary, Shelby, shoved some documents at him.

"The conference call's up," she said. "They just started the roll call."

"God, I haven't even seen the final draft of the settlement agreement," Andrew said.

"It's right here—the changes are red-lined. It's just little stuff."

"Thanks," Andrew said, "that's great."

"Do you need me anymore?" Shelby asked.

Andrew would have liked her to stay, but if a secretary worked overtime, the charges had to be billed to a client, and Andrew was meticulous about not padding bills. "No," he said, "it's six-thirty. Go home."

"You're the boss," Shelby said, but Andrew was already down the hall.

"Hi, Rachel," Andrew said to another associate who was putting on her coat as she walked.

"Hi, Andy. I'm late. I've got to pick up Amy from her afterschool, but I need to talk to you about that Hansen thing."

"I'm late too. Call me later. You know I'll be here."

"You got it."

"Oh, and tell Amy I love her artwork. It's on my wall."

Andrew rushed into his office, quickly scanned the agreement, and punched on the speakerphone on his desk. A conference operator was calling the roll.

"Edward Hargreave, representing the Lloyd Management Corporation?"

"Present."

Andrew knew that the call was going to be long and tedious, and he had learned to make the best use of his time, so while the operator continued with the roll, he dialed his mother on another line. While the phone rang, Andrew just drifted, relaxed, calm, confident. An office is often a reflection of its occupant's personality, and this was certainly true for Andrew's. The room itself was simple, modern corporate, plain but functional, with a few pieces of contemporary furniture. Everything was neat and orderly, papers arranged precisely, desktop clear except for the files for the cases he was currently working on, a computer within easy reach with neat plastic files of floppy disks beside it. There were models of sailboats—remnants of his youth, when he had worked at a yacht club in the summers so he could get in sailing time and had built models of great sailboats in the winters—on the low bookcase in front of the window. His walls were covered with art, much of it by his lover, but there was also a piece by Rachel's daughter, Amy. It was a self-portrait of a sunny five-year-old with paper legs that dangled beneath. It was a picture that a child would give to a family member as a gift, and Amy considered Andrew family. Often, at least as often as Andrew had time to, he and Miguel took care of Amy for a Sunday afternoon so Rachel could have some time for herself. Andrew loved those Sunday afternoons spent at the zoo or in the park, or, occasionally, at the movies, though Andrew was more strict about what a five-year-old should watch. Maybe we can do something this Sunday, Andrew thought—

"Hello," someone said.

"Hi, Mom. It's me."

"Andy! This is a surprise. How are you, dear?"

"I'm fine," Andrew said. "Better than fine. Everything's going great—"

On the speaker he heard someone mention indemnification. "Hold on, Mom," he said.

He pushed a button on his phone. "Wait," he said. "We didn't agree on that. There's no way my client will go along."

"Who's this?" a voice said.

"Andrew Beckett," Andrew said. "Hi, Ed. Sorry I interrupted, but we can't go along with that. I thought we had an agreement."

"Point taken. I'll see what we can do."

"Thanks," Andrew said. He punched back to his mother. "I saw Dr. Gillman today. My blood work is *excellent*. T-cells are steady, platelets are fine. . . . Hold on a sec, Mom."

He punched back to the conference call. "Yes," he said, "I think we could go along with that, though I'll have to talk to my client. Write it up and fax it to me. I'll look at it tonight and get back to you tomorrow."

He connected his mother again.

"Are you on one of those conference calls again?" she asked. "You know I hate it when you put me on hold."

Andrew laughed. "You know how boring these things are. I needed someone intelligent to talk to."

"Flattery will get you everywhere, Andy. So how is Miguel?"

"He's fine. He worries too much, like you, but he's fine."

"You know it's because we love you, Andy."

"That's what he keeps saying."

"So when are we going to see you two?" his mother asked.

"Soon," Andrew said, "soon."

———

Andrew was still at the office at 11:30 that evening. The senior partner of a large New York City law firm once was asked how he could justify paying someone right out of law school a starting salary of $70,000 per year. He responded that even at $100,000 a first-year associate would be profitable. Andrew was *very* profitable. The economics are simple: A good associate can bill $350,000 per year, or an associate like Andrew even more, much more. Take up to a third of that for his or her salary, a third more for office overhead, and that still leaves more than $100,000 to be distributed to the partners. Obviously, the more associates there are per partner, the more profit the partners make, which is the main reason that so few associates are asked to become partners; even many very good ones are told at the end of their stint of seven or eight years that their services are no longer required.

Andrew knew the economics, and he knew that the more time he billed the better chance he had of being made a partner, but that was not why he worked the long hours that he did. He worked that hard because he loved the way it felt. He loved the law and its arcane complexities; he loved the fact that occasionally a case came along where he was not just a hired gun protecting some monolithic corporation but was actually able to help correct an injustice. He loved his particular field, corporate litigation, because he loved the constant challenge of creating strategy that had to change on a moment's notice in response to another lawyer's actions, and he loved the challenge of having to think quickly and clearly in a courtroom. Knowledgeable associates tried to stay away from litigation. An associate in general corporate law or in tax who was passed over for partner generally found a good job—although not as highly paid—in the legal department of a large corporation, sometimes even a corporation that was a client of the former associate's law firm. However, since most corporations entrust litigation to outside firms, there are many fewer corporate positions for passed-over associates in litigation, and when a job is found there is usually a large salary contraction, as it is euphemistically called. Andrew did not care, however; his future seemed secure at Wyant, Wheeler, and even if he thought his future would be more promising in another specialty, he would not have changed.

Wyant, Wheeler's general library looked like law libraries everywhere: functional, not luxurious, clearly intended for serious research, not socializing or relaxing. With its comfortable, modern armchairs and the small, red-shaded reading lamps on each table, it might have been just a bit more luxurious than libraries in other firms, but basically it was designed for work, which was exactly what Andrew was doing at 11:30 that night. He *knew* there was a case directly on the point he was researching, and he was going to find it.

As Andrew worked, Mr. Seidman walked quietly down the hall and then stopped and watched from the door, but Andrew was too engrossed to notice his presence, and for a few minutes Mr. Seidman just stood and watched, reflecting on his own days as a young lawyer. He had graduated from law school at the height of the Vietnam war and his employment at Wyant, Wheeler was entered into with a bit of reluctance by both parties. Mr. Seidman had insisted as a condition of his employment that he be allowed to spend part of his time on *pro bono publico* work, which was not a major priority at Wyant, Wheeler. Nevertheless, he had graduated at the top of his class at Harvard, and Wyant,

Wheeler wanted him. Although the relationship got off to a rough start, Mr. Seidman's brilliance and intellect soon won him friends and allies among the partners. Now, he thought, he had really made it, and Andrew Beckett was going to follow in his footsteps.

Andrew looks tired, Mr. Seidman thought. I wonder if we're working him too hard. But then he remembered his own associate years and how hard he had worked. He knew it was just part of the position, something you did to increase your chances of being named a partner.

Andrew stopped his work long enough to reach for a sautéed string bean from a take-out carton—at the same time hearing Dr. Gillman's voice saying, I know you work hard, but you *must* eat—and then turned back to the library computer that was connected to all the legal databases.

"Eureka!" he said. "I knew you were there. Sulike versus Southwest National Bank. The court of appeals *affirmed* the jury award of punitive damages for wrongful interference with prospective economic relations."

Andrew scrolled through the decision and then turned to his notebook computer and typed quickly. Mr. Seidman moved closer and closer until he was standing directly behind Andrew, but Andrew did not even look up.

"Andy," Mr. Seidman said, "am I interrupting?"

Andrew still did not look up. "In a word, Bob, yes."

"Charles would like to see you upstairs."

When a name partner asks to see an associate, the associate is always free. "I was just about to take a break,"

Andrew said, and he turned toward Mr. Seidman who, he was surprised to see, was wearing black-tie evening clothes. The partners must have had some social function, Andrew thought. "You're sure I'm not underdressed?" he asked, since his jacket was back in his office and he was in shirtsleeves and suspenders.

"You're fine," Mr. Seidman said, and Andrew got up and followed him to Mr. Wheeler's office, wondering what was going on that late at night.

Although the offices in associate territory were plain and functional, Mr. Wheeler's office—jokingly referred to by associates and some of the bolder staff as Valhalla—was anything but. It was huge, with a long, rich leather couch in front of floor-to-ceiling windows that looked out over the Philadelphia skyline; carefully placed leather armchairs and mahogany end tables holding expensive lamps; Oriental rugs scattered on top of thick carpeting; glassware and heavy crystal decanters on a side table. It was an office that said its occupant was successful, solid, conservative, powerful.

All four of the firm's senior partners were gathered there, all wearing flawlessly pressed tuxedos and snow-white, perfectly starched shirts. Obviously, something important was up, Andrew thought: Killcoyne, Kenton, Seidman, and Wheeler all in the office at midnight. As far as Andrew knew, it had never happened before, and if it had, they certainly had not wanted to meet with a mere associate. Andrew looked from face to face: Wheeler—smug, supremely self-confident, a great and innovative lawyer yet somehow, Andrew thought, not completely trustworthy; Kenton—aggressive, unfeeling, with a reputation for meanness, although he had always treated Andrew well; Killcoyne, whose obsequiousness to Wheeler was obvious to everyone. Although Andrew was usually self-confident, something about the scene made him nervous, and he looked out the windows to collect his thoughts for a moment. The windows overlooked the central part of the city, and the tall, lighted buildings reminded Andrew a bit of New York, but New York, he thought, could never be quite this beautiful.

The partners already had cognac, and Mr. Wheeler was passing around a box of large cigars. "Cigar, Andy?" he asked, and Andrew turned his thoughts back to the room. Was he about to be rewarded? An early partnership, perhaps?

"Thank you," Andrew said, and he took a cigar from the box, and examined it.

When everyone was seated and everyone, except Andrew, had lit their cigars and was puffing away contentedly, Mr. Seidman started the conversation.

"Charles," he said to Mr. Wheeler, "Andrew has expressed an interest in Highline, Inc. versus Sander Systems. Isn't that right, Andrew?"

This could be trouble. Andrew mentally reviewed what he knew about the case; hundreds of millions—and probably ten million in legal fees—were at stake.

"Yes, sir, the fate of the participants interests me," he said carefully.

Mr. Wheeler seemed not to hear the response, and he picked up his cognac, leaned back in his chair, and exhaled several perfect rings of smoke in Andrew's direction. The smoke bothered Andrew, but he did not pull back.

"It's good to be king, hey, Charles?" Mr. Kenton said.

Mr. Wheeler looked as though he could easily play the part of a king, with his silver hair and distinguished nose. "Why, Walter," he said, "you know kings are out of fashion these days after the Brits have made such a mess of it. I'd rather be thought of as a benevolent tyrant."

The partners all chuckled and laughed approvingly. Andrew laughed too, but his laughter concealed tension.

Mr. Wheeler turned his attention to Andrew. "The Highline case is an antitrust action," he prompted.

"Well, Charles, it is and it isn't," Andrew replied. "Sander System's new spreadsheet program copies all the best-known elements of Highline's, even down to some of the icons used on the screen. If a giant like Sander gets away with it, Highline will get undersold right out of business."

Everyone was paying close attention, and Andrew thought for a moment; he was about to disagree with Charles Wheeler. "For me," he said, "the legal principle involved is more copyright infringement than antitrust."

The partners all watched carefully, but no one said anything; everyone watched Mr. Wheeler.

"Tell me, Andy," he finally said, "which side of this conflict would you like to see emerge victorious?"

"I—" Andrew started to speak, but Mr. Wheeler interrupted him, and as he did Mr. Kenton put on his glasses and stared at Andrew's face.

"—And don't let my personal relationship, my *close* personal relationship, with Bill Wright, Sander System's CEO, influence your answer in any way."

Right, Andrew thought. He, and the others, knew this was a test, and he considered his answer carefully.

Andrew took a breath. "Candidly, Charles," he said, "I'd love to see Highline win this one."

"Why, Beckett?" Mr. Kenton asked. It was not a friendly question.

"Because they deserve to, Walter," Andrew said. He was perspiring, and when he wiped his face he discovered that his hair was back, which he knew revealed the small lesion on his forehead. He casually rearranged his hair with his hand.

"That's it? Because they deserve to?" Mr. Seidman asked.

"If Sander Systems wins, an energetic, young company will be destroyed. Moreover, the laws of copyright—*and* antitrust"—he smiled at Mr. Wheeler—"were enacted to protect against exactly the kind of bullshit that Sander Systems is trying to pull."

"Andy, do you know who represents Highline?" Mr. Seidman asked.

"Rodney Bailey—"

" 'I object!' Rodney Bailey," Mr. Seidman interjected.

Andrew nodded. "Rodney Bailey, who couldn't find his way around copyright law with a map and a guide."

Everyone was quiet. Mr. Wheeler was enjoying this. He took a long pull on his cigar, swirled the cognac in his glass, and blew another smoke ring. "Apparently, the fellas at Highline agree with you, which explains why, as of eleven-fifteen this evening—right after the dessert course, I might add—Highline Inc. is now represented by Wyant, Wheeler, Hellerman, Tetlow, and Brown."

Mr. Wheeler paused, then continued, "Or, more specifically, by senior associate Andrew Beckett."

Andrew knew he should simply say thank you, but he was so excited he raised his fists in a victory salute and yelled, "Yes," which made the partners all smile at each other. They had all felt the same way at some time in their lives when there was great personal achievement.

"You'll have to get on it right away," Mr. Seidman said.

"Right," Andrew said. "We're up against the statute of limitations here. And—"

He was interrupted by a ringing telephone. "Tokyo for you on four, Bob," Mr. Killcoyne said.

"This could be the call we've been waiting for," Mr. Seidman said. "Excuse me."

"I hope Rodney Bailey's secretary brings him a pacemaker with his morning coffee tomorrow," Mr. Killcoyne said, and then everyone stood and offered congratulations. Associates, even senior associates, were almost never given control over cases this large; there was too much at risk in reputation, and in future legal fees, if the firm lost. This was the high point of Andrew's young career, and they all knew it and gathered around to shake his hand.

Mr. Kenton alone was not effusive. Instead he studied Andrew's face, and when Andrew extended his hand to him, Mr. Kenton ignored it and said, "What's that on your forehead, Pal?"

"Whacked with a racquetball," Andrew said, casually brushing his hair down with one hand. He turned to Mr. Wheeler. "Charles," he said, "I sincerely appreciate your faith in my abilities."

Mr. Kenton ignored the celebratory goings-on and continued to stare at Andrew.

"Faith," Mr. Wheeler said with great self-importance, "is the belief in something for which we have no evidence. It does not apply in this situation. Now go home. I mean, get back to work."

Andrew looked around the office again and then out at the spectacular view of the Philadelphia skyline at night and he was incredibly happy. In the elation of the moment he did not think about his illness, he did not think about medications and doctors and hospitals, he did not think of dying. He thought of life.

"Thanks again," he said quietly.

"No sweat, Buddy," Mr. Wheeler said, also quietly, "you deserved it."

It took Andrew great effort to leave the office with dignity, and as soon as he was in the hall he erupted, dancing as though he'd scored a touchdown, and then boxed his way down the hall like a prizefighter. A cleaning lady laughed at the exhibition, and Andrew took the cigar from his pocket and put it in his mouth and said, "Ah, Helena, it *is* good to be king."

"Mr. Beckett," the cleaning lady said, "you are definitely crazy. Those long hours have finally gotten to you."

Two

The progress of the disease called AIDS defies explanation or prediction. Patients can go for several years with only minor problems and then become seriously ill overnight. One of the subsidiary infections the destruction of the body's immune system allows is a painful, brutal, ravaging cancer called Kaposi's sarcoma, referred to almost universally but certainly not affectionately as KS. It causes lesions—sores—on the skin and is also unpredictable. A patient can have KS for years with only a spot or two on the body, and then almost overnight the cancer blossoms and spreads, as it did with Andrew. Two weeks after he was awarded the Highline case, the lesion on his forehead had become four, all of them ugly, disfiguring.

He first noticed them on a Sunday morning as he was getting ready to go to brunch with his lover.

"Miguel," he called from the bathroom, "you'd better come in here."

Andrew was the early riser in the family; Miguel never seemed to wake up much before noon. Andrew always said he felt sorry for students in Miguel's morning classes.

"Give me five minutes," Miguel called from the bed.

Andrew shook his head and wrapped a towel around himself and went outside and turned on the light.

"Ouch," Miguel said.

"Look at this," Andrew said. He pulled his wet hair back and held it with his hand.

"Oh, honey," Miguel said. He got up and looked at Andrew's face closely, then put his arms around him.

"I can't go to work like this," Andrew said. "What am I going to do?"

"Why don't you go on leave, live a little. You'd still get more than half pay, and we don't need the money anyway." Miguel rubbed Andrew's back and added, "Please, Drew."

"You know I can't do that," Andrew said. He kissed Miguel lightly on the forehead and went to the window. God, he loved this city. Their building was higher than the buildings around it, and their loft looked out over blocks of rooftops to the skyscrapers of the central city. He could even see the Wheeler building, a monolith of marble and glass, and he could see the clock tower on top of city hall, which was for many years the highest point in Philadelphia.

"Drew," Miguel said, "come here."

Andrew did not move or speak, and Miguel came to the window and put his arms around Andrew's waist from behind. "We're going to beat this," he said. "I just wish you'd stop working so hard."

"You don't understand," Andrew said. "I *like* working. That's what keeps me alive. If I stopped working I wouldn't last three months."

"Drew, can you at least work at home for a while? We can set up an office for you here and that way you can rest when you need to."

"It looks like I'm going to have to," Andrew said. "I can't go to work looking like this."

Their loft had always been a comfortable home, with its hardwood floors polished to a warm, brown glow and the accents of red in the furniture that added even more warmth. But over the next few days their loft became a working law office as well, complete with a fax machine, a small copy machine, a speakerphone with three lines, a large personal computer, and Andrew's notebook computer. The Highline motion papers and briefs were going well, thanks to the help of several of Andrew's friends who got books from the library, acted as messengers, and generally helped out in whatever way they could. That particular morning there was more confusion than usual because not only were there three friends in the apartment, but the Highline papers had to be filed by 5:00 that afternoon, and in addition to last-minute instructions Andrew was trying to give to various people at his office, Andrew's friend Chandra was trying to teach him how to use makeup to conceal the lesions on his face. Although it was warm in the apartment Andrew had complained that he was cold, and he wore a heavy sweater over a long-sleeved shirt.

"Well, guys," Andrew said, "it looks as though we did it. The revisions are on my desk, and we're serving the papers by five."

"*You* did it," Andrew's friend Bruno called from across the room, where he was channel surfing with the TV remote. "We just did the running around for you."

"Well, anyway, I appreciate it," Andrew said.

"Just let me check in with the office one more time, and then I can concentrate on that junk you want to put on my face," he told Chandra, who had jars of makeup spread across the table.

Andrew pushed a speed-dial button and tried to keep Chandra's hand away from his face.

"Hi, Shelby," Andrew said into the speakerphone. "We're ready to roll. The revised complaint is in my out box. Make sure Jamey's on top of it."

"Hold still," Chandra said.

"Who's that?" Shelby asked.

"Just a friend," Andrew said. He pushed Chandra's hand away again. "Anyway, please make sure Jamey files those papers today. Don't let him wait until the last minute."

"Okay," Shelby said. "Is there anything else you need me to do?"

"That's it. I'll be working at home for the rest of the day. Thanks, Shelby."

Andrew clicked off the phone. "Okay, Chandra, let's get this over with," he said.

"Hold on," Chandra said. "Your sweater's going to be a mess. Alan, get me a towel."

"At your service," Alan said. Alan was a proofreader on the night shift at another law firm, so he was able to help Andrew during the days, and his help had been invaluable. He brought a towel from the bathroom and draped it around Andrew's neck, over his sweater. As Chandra started to work on the makeup, the fax machine started humming, and Andrew pushed Chandra's hand away.

"Sit still," she said. "Bruno," she added, "get that fax, will you?"

Chandra did the makeup for the news shows on one of the local television stations, and she knew how to make it look natural. "You want to apply the foundation as evenly as you can, Andy. You don't want to look like you've thrown it on with a trowel," Chandra said as she put the makeup on Andrew's face.

"Where's that fax?" Andrew said.

"Coming," Bruno said, running over with the curled paper. He was a slight man for such an imposing name.

"Are you listening to me?" Chandra asked.

"I'm trying," Andrew said. He scanned the fax quickly. It was a confirmation of his instructions. "Jamey's okay," he said to himself.

"Okay," Chandra said, "let's see what you've learned. You try." She handed Andrew a brush, and he started putting on the makeup himself, looking into a mirror standing on the table in front of him.

"Chandra," he said, "don't you think this color's a little too orange for me?"

"It's Tahitian bronze. It works best on lesions."

"Think of it as the I-just-got-back-from-Aruba look," Alan said.

"I've called in sick for four days," Andrew said. "I don't want them to think I've been to the beach or something." He looked back in the mirror and then tried on several pairs of sunglasses, finally settling on a pair with big tortoiseshell frames. "Check this out. Hides everything, right? What do you think?"

Chandra studied him for a moment. "You know who you look like? That actor, in that movie. Not the one where he was autistic, the one where he dressed up like a lady to get a part in a soap opera."

"Dustin Hoffman," Bruno said.

"Yeah," Chandra agreed.

"I look like Tootsie!" Andrew said with horror.

"Right," Bruno told him.

"You want to try light Egyptian?" Chandra asked.

"I'll try—" Andrew started, and suddenly he felt terribly ill, with a sharp pain in his stomach. "Excuse me a sec," he said, and he stood and bent over, holding himself. He started walking toward the bathroom, obviously in pain, and then he started to run and when he got there, he slammed the door hard behind him.

"Just like my cousin Fredo," Chandra said sadly. They were all quiet, and then another of Andrew's friends, Peter, came in with a shopping bag full of food. "Anybody want a bagel?" he asked, and no one answered. Peter looked at their faces and then put the bag on the table.

"Somebody better see how he is," Chandra said.

Bruno knocked on the bathroom door. "Andy, are you all right?"

Andrew didn't answer.

Bruno tried the door, but it was locked. "Andy!" he called. "Talk to me. Are you all right?"

"I think I need to go to the hospital," Andrew said weakly from inside.

There was immediate confusion. Chandra said she'd get Andrew's coat; Alan was on the phone asking information for the number for the Academy of Fine Arts, where Miguel taught painting; Bruno tried to get into the bathroom, but the door was still locked and Andrew was in too much pain to get up and unlock it. "Andy," Bruno called, "I'm going to break this door down with something if you can't unlock it."

"I'm coming," Andrew said. There was the sound of water running in the sink, and then the door opened slowly. Andrew looked terrible. He was perspiring heavily and the makeup had already started to run.

"Jesus," Bruno said, "what happened?"

"I don't know, just call me a cab, please. And give me your arm."

"Okay, you're a cab," Bruno said.

Andrew tried to smile, but he was feeling too weak. He took Bruno's arm and slowly made his way out into the main room, where Chandra was waiting with his coat.

"Oh God, you look awful," she said.

"The cab's on its way, and Miguel's meeting us there," Alan said.

"Thanks," Andy said to no one in particular. "Oh," he said, "could someone please call Dr. Gillman for me? The number's in that card file by the phone."

There could not have been a worse time for this, Andrew thought. The Highline brief is due out today, I've got an apartment full of people, and Miguel is at school. I wonder if this will be the time, he thought with a rush of fear, the time when I go to the hospital, something happens, and I don't come home. He looked around the loft, a large, airy, light-filled room with a wall of windows, remembering when he and Miguel had first moved here, remembering Miguel's delight at the abundant natural light that he needed for his painting, remembering the fun of buying furniture, painting walls, fixing things themselves. And before that, there was the first night they spent here, the night after they closed on the sale when Miguel said, "Let's just have dinner there, and then we can sleep at the old place," the night when he came in from work to find the loft lit with candlelight and filled with flowers, a mattress on the floor, and a few essentials Miguel had brought over during the day. The night they ate dinner by candlelight and then sat by the windows looking at the lights of the city and then made gentle love. The night Miguel said, "We're home, Baby."

———

Hospital emergency rooms are cold—literally—and impersonal places. Emergency room doctors are often young residents who try to be caring, but are exhausted after day after day of shifts that often exceed fifteen hours. Nurses, usually with more emergency room experience than the doctors themselves, try to keep things under control, but frequently they have to leave one patient abruptly for a new one who is more in need of immediate care. For the staff's convenience—but certainly not the patient's—hospitals usually insist that patients who are going to require any kind of test wear one of those absurd hospital gowns that conceal little and rob an already concerned and sometimes confused patient of what little dignity he or she has left. Unlike most patients, Andrew was lucky. He came into the emergency room with an entire phalanx of friends who were prepared to be as assertive as necessary. And their assertiveness *was* necessary from the moment they arrived.

First, Andrew had to see a triage nurse, who was responsible for determining exactly how seriously ill incoming patients were and assigning care accordingly. Unfortunately, the triage nurse on duty was gossiping with her colleagues about a movie that she had seen the night before and after a quick look at Andrew, she directed him to a chair and told him to wait and went back to her conversation.

"Excuse me!" Bruno said. "Is anyone on duty here?"

The nurse who was interrupted turned around and said, "You're not supposed to be in here. Wait for your friend outside." She walked around a partition out of sight, and continued her conversation.

"I'll be all right," Andrew said, but Bruno ignored him and followed the nurse. "My friend needs help *now*," he told her.

The nurse was a young woman, a little heavy, not very attractive, and she had already decided that Andrew was not in danger of dying in the immediate future. "Sir, if you don't get out of here I'm going to call security," the nurse told Bruno.

"And if you don't get out here and take care of my friend *I'm* going to find an administrator and complain," Bruno said. "Sweetheart," he added.

"You'd better go take a look," one of the other nurses told her.

"Wait outside," she said to Bruno, but finally Andrew got some attention. He was sitting in a chair holding his shoulders with his arms crossed across his chest, shivering so badly his teeth were chattering. Without speaking, the nurse held out an electronic thermometer and then watched a digital display on a little black box while Andrew held the probe in his mouth. The numbers kept going up: 99, 100, 100.4, 100.7, 101, 101.3, 101.5, 101.6, 101.7, 101.7, 101.7. The box beeped when the numbers did not increase any more and the nurse said, as if surprised, "You're hot!"

"I'm cold too," Andrew said. "May I please have a blanket?" He felt miserable. The pain in his abdomen had receded, but he could not shake the chills. All he wanted to do was see Miguel and lie down somewhere and go to sleep.

"We'll get you one once we get you processed," the nurse said.

"Listen," Andrew said. He tried hard to concentrate and to be polite. "I really am cold, and I could really use a blanket. I'll just wrap it around me."

The nurse considered his request for a moment and then called to an aide to bring a blanket. "You'll have to put on a gown before you see a doctor, anyway," the nurse told Andrew.

She then took Andrew's blood pressure and asked for some basic medical information. When she was finished, she directed Andrew down the hall to Emergency Room Admitting. Her last words to Andrew were "Don't walk away with that blanket, now."

Alan, Chandra, and Bruno were waiting outside the triage area. "Where'd they get her?" Bruno said. "She should be emptying trash or something. Not seeing patients."

Andrew was always the peacemaker (he often said the best lawsuits were ones that didn't happen) and in spite of his aggravating encounter with the nurse he said, "Would you like her job? She doesn't really get to treat patients, all she does is listen to an endless stream of people complain about what's wrong with them, day after day after day. She deserves to vent a little."

"I'll have her job," Bruno said.

"You wouldn't look good in that uniform," Andrew said.

"I meant—"

"Never mind, you two," Chandra interrupted. "Dr. Gillman's not in her office today."

"Miguel's on his way," Alan said.

"Thank you all," Andrew said. "I just need to get myself admitted or whatever and lie down."

The woman in the admitting office could not have been kinder or more compassionate. "You don't look so good," she said. "Why don't you just sit down over there and I'll get the information I need from your friends."

Andrew nodded gratefully, wrapped his blanket tightly around himself, and huddled on a chair while his friends helped the clerk with the forms. Andrew had to get up once to hand over his insurance card, and then after a few minutes more the clerk snapped a tape around his wrist and called for a doctor herself. By then Andrew had been there for more than thirty minutes and had not yet received any care. That thirty minutes was a short wait by emergency room standards—without the intervention of his friends it would have been much longer. And now there were new ordeals. Andrew did not want to wear a gown, and he managed to convince another nurse that he would put one on when and if it was necessary. The doctor thought Andrew's respiration rate was too high, and he not only ordered a battery of routine blood tests but he also ordered a test that required blood from an artery. It is a painful procedure: A small needle is forced deep into the wrist at the point where the pulse can be felt. Andrew hated the needles; they were, he said, the worst thing about having AIDS, worse even than the possibility of dying. Nevertheless, when all the necessary blood was finally drawn, he thanked the technician, truly grateful he had been so skillful. Then the doctor wanted specimens and came back several times asking further questions about Andrew's recent medical history. Through it all Andrew was worrying about whether the Highline brief would be served on time, and then his beeper sounded. It will have to wait, Andrew thought, and he shut it off, seeing Miguel rush in the door. Andrew smiled and even before Miguel reached him he began to relax and then Miguel put his arm around Andrew and Andrew squeezed his hand and for an instant Andrew thought, I am so lucky.

"God, I'm glad you're here," Andrew said. "Dr. Gillman's out of her office today. Can you believe it, I tell her to take a day off and she does."

"That's okay," Miguel said. He put his hand on

Andrew's forehead. "You're hot," he said. "Did they take blood?"

"Lots."

"A specimen?"

Andrew picked up an empty specimen cup and showed it to Miguel. "Did you get someone to cover your class?" he asked.

"Don't worry about it," Miguel said, and he kissed Andrew's forehead, and Andrew leaned into him and he could not be brave any longer and tears started to come. "I almost didn't make it," he told Miguel. "I almost lost it right there in front of everyone." He leaned into Miguel and Miguel held him tightly and said, "So what? Don't worry about it. You have nothing to be ashamed of, nothing. Okay?"

Andrew rubbed away the tears and pulled himself together and squeezed Miguel's hand again, and for a moment neither of them said anything, and then Miguel took his hand away and started looking around the room, all business now. He was here and he and Andrew were going to get some answers.

"Where's your doctor?" he asked.

Andrew pointed to a young resident rushing by. "Hey," he called. "That's my guy," he told Miguel. "Hey!" he called again to the doctor.

Being a patient in an emergency room is not a pleasant experience, but being a physician in one is not pleasant either. Young residents who work for little more than slave wages and who often have had little sleep for days on end are required to make decision after decision about patients they have never seen before. Some of the required decisions, if made incorrectly, can result in death—and a lawsuit—and while other decisions, like what tests to order, seem simpler, the doctor often does not know which ones might be crucial. In the thirty minutes after he first saw Andrew, the young doctor caring for him had stitched up a jagged, bloody wound—caused by a broken bottle—in the scalp of a raving drunk who had wanted to kill the doctor for touching him. Then the doctor had revived a baby who was not breathing. Andrew was not at the top of his list of priorities.

"Hey," Andrew said again.

"Oh—" The doctor paused to remember the name. "—Mr. Beckett. I'm sorry. It's been a busy day."

Miguel took out a little notebook he had bought shortly after Andrew had become ill. It had flowers on the cover, and on some of the pages he had made simple line sketches of Andrew, of doctors, of technicians, and on other pages there was writing. In a way, the writing in that little book told a story that by now has been repeated hundreds of thousands of times around the world: It did not contain any elegant prose; the characters, including Andrew, were just names with no personalities. It told its story with the simple recitation of dates, lab results, medications taken, medications considered, medications refused, symptoms observed, physicians consulted; and now the resident caring for Andrew was about to have a few lines of his own.

"What about my blood work?" Andrew asked.

"We're waiting for the lab," the resident said. "Meanwhile, I'd like to prepare you for a colonoscopy so we can take a look inside."

Andrew made a face. "That sounds just delightful," he said. "The perfect end to a perfect day."

"Why do you need to do that?" Miguel demanded.

Andrew's beeper sounded again and he quickly shut it off.

"Who are you?" the resident asked Miguel.

Miguel had inherited some of the stereotypical hot Mediterranean temperament and in matters concerning Andrew he did little to control it. "Who am *I*?" he said. "Just exactly who are *you*, Doctor?"

Oh God, Andrew thought, the last thing I need now is a fight. He remembered a screaming argument in Spanish when an inexperienced lab technician had had to stick Andrew more than once to draw blood: *Andrew* had had to comfort *Miguel*, and it had taken fifteen minutes to get Miguel calm again.

Andrew put his hand on Miguel's arm and said to the resident, "This is my partner. We keep records of all medical procedures. It's nothing personal."

Just what I need, the resident thought, I'm going to be sued. "I'm Dr. Klenstein," he said to Miguel.

"You're right," he said to Andrew, "it's not a pleasant procedure, but if the KS is causing the diarrhea we ought to know right away."

"Yes, but it could also be parasites, or an infection," Miguel said.

"Or a reaction to AZT," Andrew added.

"That's possible," Dr. Klenstein admitted, "but—"

"He's not going through some painful procedure until we've eliminated *everything* else," Miguel said loudly.

"Look," Dr. Klenstein told him, "I'm just trying to help your 'partner.' You're not a member of his immediate family."

"I'm not?!" Miguel yelled.

"Listen," Dr. Klenstein said, "I could have you removed from the ER."

"*You're* going to have *me* removed?"

"Miguel," Andrew said.

"He's upset," Andrew told Dr. Klenstein. "He's sorry."

"Don't apologize for me," Miguel said.

"Okay, fine, he's not sorry," Andrew said. "Why don't we see what we find out from the blood work first, and I'll work on getting a specimen. Maybe by then we'll hear from my own doctor, and we can go from there. Does that make everybody happy?"

"All right," Dr. Klenstein said. "I'll try to get the lab to speed up the results on the blood work."

"Thank you," Miguel said.

Dr. Klenstein just nodded.

"I'm sorry," Miguel added.

Dr. Klenstein nodded again, and as he walked away Andrew's beeper sounded again.

"That's the third time they've beeped me," he told Miguel. "I'd better call the office."

"Will you please forget about your office," Miguel said. "I just want you to get better."

"I'm just going to make one call. Look on the bright side: At least my ass isn't hanging out; they didn't make me wear one of those damned gowns."

"I wish you'd forget about the office," Miguel demanded.

"One call, Miguel. Would you please relax."

"I am relaxed," he said.

"Fine. Just wait for me right here in case the doc comes back. I'll be right over there." He pointed to the waiting room.

"One call," Miguel said.

The pay phones were firmly bolted on a rack high on the wall, near a television that was being watched by a group of weary, concerned friends and relatives of patients inside. As Andrew searched for a quarter and then dialed, a commercial for Joe Miller's law firm came on, and Andrew heard Joe's voice. "If you or someone you know has been injured through the fault of others, you may be entitled to a cash settlement for your pain and suffering."

Andrew looked up at the image on the screen. The background was a succession of photos of smiling clients, some in wheelchairs or wearing casts, holding up checks for the camera.

Andrew laughed, and then his secretary answered.

"Shelby. It's me. Someone's been beeping me. What's up?"

"Oh my God, we've got a terrible problem. I don't know what to do. Jamey and I've been . . . it's terrible." Shelby sounded as though she was about to cry.

"Calm down. It can't be that bad. Put Jamey on."

Be calm, Andrew thought, be calm. Whatever it is can be solved.

"Andy," Jamey said, "this is a disaster! We can't find the final draft of the Highline complaint! I went down to word processing to pick up the corrected copy, but they said you didn't deliver the corrections. I *told* those people that I was sure you'd sent it in, but they say they haven't seen it!"

"Calm down," Andrew said. "I brought it into the office last night and then worked on it there until three a.m. As I explained this morning, I left the final draft in my out box with a note to you and Shelby."

"There's nothing here either. I figured the mailroom picked it up and took it to word processing like they should have, but its not there either. Oh God, what are we going to do?"

Andrew knew that the important thing was not to

worry about what had already happened but to serve the complaint on time, and he had to get Jamey to do that. "All right, Jamey, listen. Sit at my computer. It's on the hard drive."

"Okay," Jamey said, "I'm here. What did you file it under?"

"H-L-one," Andrew said. "The subdirectory is called high, that's spelled h-i-g-h." Andrew could hear keys clicking furiously. "I don't need to mention, do I, that the complaint has to be filed"—he looked at his watch—"in exactly seventy-five minutes."

"It's not here," Jamey yelled. "There is no 'high' subdirectory."

This was serious. A computer file can be accidentally put in the wrong place on a hard drive, perhaps through a typo, but an entire directory cannot disappear without performing several steps in a specific order.

"Never mind the computer," Andrew said. "You go down to word processing and tell those jerk-offs they better come up with that complaint now, or they are *fucking dead*! And you tell them that comes from me!" Andrew was shouting now, and Jamey tried to interrupt. "*Now!*" Andrew yelled, and he slammed down the phone.

"Shit!" he said. "Shit!" People in the waiting room looked up nervously. Calm down, Andrew told himself, calm down. Every problem has a solution. Solution or not, he half ran back to Miguel.

"What's going on?" Miguel asked.

Andrew did not answer but took off the blanket and began fixing his shirt and looking around for the rest of his things.

"What's wrong?" Miguel asked. "Why are you getting dressed?"

Andrew stopped and put his arm around Miguel. "Listen," he said, "you're not going to like this, and thanks for leaving your budding Picassos and coming here for me"—Andrew pulled away and started putting on his jacket—"and I *will* be back. One hour. Tops. I promise."

"You're going to the office!"

"You're not smiling, Miguel."

"You are *not* going to the office, Drew. You are going to stay here until they find out what's wrong with you."

"One hour, Miguel," Andrew said, and he kissed Miguel on the cheek. Before Miguel could say anything more, Andrew rushed out of the hospital, leaving Miguel totally defeated and almost in tears, and ignoring the nurse who yelled "Hey!" as the doors closed behind him. He hopped in a cab that was letting off a man with one arm wrapped in a bloody towel and told the driver it was worth a twenty if he would really hurry.

"Usually people are in a hurry to get to the hospital, not get away from it," the driver said.

"Drive!" Andrew said. He was in shock. Was it possible that all of the hard work he had done could come undone so suddenly?

The driver looked in his mirror and got a clear look at Andrew's face and said no more. He drove. The faster I get there, he thought, the faster I get this leper out of my cab.

Andrew knew he looked bad—although he did not realize just how bad—so he pulled the brim of his baseball cap low over his forehead and directed the driver to the Wheeler service entrance, which was in an underground garage. He snuck into his law firm like a thief: up in a dirty service elevator, out into the firm's kitchen, down through a dimly lit service corridor, through the main hall, ducking into a doorway when anyone approached. Finally, though, he had to go out in the open, so he tucked his head down and walked directly to his office, and he could not avoid meeting Rachel, whose daughter had made the self-portrait that hung in Andrew's office.

"Andy! My God, what are you doing here? Someone might see you!" Rachel walked beside Andrew until he reached his office, where he found his secretary and Jamey frantically searching through papers on his desk. Andrew pulled his hat down more and turned partially toward the wall.

"Did you find it yet?" Andrew demanded as he slammed the door.

"We've got nothing, Andy," Jamey said.

"Shelby, call the messenger service and have someone standing by," Andrew ordered.

Shelby reached for Andrew's phone while still staring at his face.

"*Your* phone," Andrew said. "Please."

"Sure," she answered. "It's here, I know it's here," she said, and she rushed out, knowing then what she had suspected for a long time.

Three

A ndrew's office was a wreck. First he went through every document he could find, throwing each to the floor when he saw that it was not the right one, ignoring the fact that soon these documents would be important too. Then he started on his files of floppy disks, slamming each one into the drive, reading the directory, sometimes viewing a file, and then frantically ripping the disk out and throwing it to the floor, where it joined the growing piles of trash. "Jesus!" Andrew yelled. "A file can't just disappear, a directory can't disappear! What's going on! I must be losing my—"

Jamey burst in without knocking. "It's nowhere," he said. "It's nowhere! We've got nothing, Andy!"

"Look, Jamey, it has to be somewhere. I *know* I was here last night. I *know* I left the hard copy on my desk and the file on my computer."

"Then where is it, Andy? Maybe you just thought you

left it here. You've been working awfully hard, and you've been sick—"

"I am not losing my mind, Jamey! It was *here*!"

"Okay, Andy, it's here someplace. But meanwhile it's four-twenty. We've got forty minutes. You've gotta tell Wheeler what's going on."

Andrew's fever was climbing, and his makeup had run, making his face streaked with brown and revealing the lesions. Talking to Charles Wheeler was something he could not think about.

"Go back to word processing and check again," he told Jamey. "Now!"

"I've been down to word processing ten times, it's—"

"Then go down to the mail room and see if anything's been—"

"Fine, I'll go. I'll do whatever you want. But if I were you I'd call Wheeler or Seidman right away!"

"And talk to housekeeping and find out who cleaned up in here. Now! And close the door behind you!"

Jamey rushed out, almost in tears, and Andrew paced. "Think!" he told himself. "Think!" He kicked at piles of paper, kicked at disks. When he missed one disk with his foot he picked it up and hurled it against the wall by the door just as Rachel came in.

"Andy!" she said. "What are you, crazy? What are you doing coming in here looking like this? Come on." Andrew had been turned away from her, and she turned him around to face her. "Oh my God, Andy, you look awful!" she said.

"Rach, I need you to go down to the mail room, and then—"

"Andy! You cannot be here looking like this. I told you, you look awful!"

"We can't find the complaint, Rach. I need your help, now!"

"Andy, never mind the complaint. We have to get you out of here!"

"Rach, *please* go to the mail room, and then down to word processing. The supervisor's giving Jamey a hard time. I want you to tell him I'll have his job if—"

"Andy, stop it!" Rachel yelled. "We have got to get you out of here."

"Please, Rach, *please*. I need your help. Now go!" Andrew turned her around and pushed her out the door and then slammed it, hard. "Think!" he said. "What did I do with that complaint?" He kicked at some papers again and then went to his desk and picked up his phone to do what he had to do, knowing that he was definitely in trouble.

"Hello, Bob here," Andy heard.

"Bob, this is Andy."

"Hi, Andy, what's up?"

"I have a little problem with the Highline complaint. I don't want to alarm you or Charles, but—"

"What happened, Andy?" Mr. Seidman asked. His voice had turned serious.

"It's . . . Oh shit, Bob, it's gotta be filed in thirty-five minutes and I've lost it. I can't find it." Andrew's voice almost broke.

"*You* lost something. I don't believe it."

"It's gone, Bob, just gone."

"Okay, okay, I'll be right down."

"No! Don't do that!" Andrew shouted, but Mr. Seidman had already hung up. "Jesus! Now what do I do!" Andrew pushed his hair back and his hand came away orange. "Jesus!" he said, and he wiped his hand on his pants and ran to the door and shut off the lights and then back to the windows and closed the blinds so the only light was from the lamp on his desk. He was just sitting down when Mr. Seidman walked in without knocking.

"C'mon, Andy," he said from the doorway, "you didn't lose anything." He looked around the dark, messy office. "And how are you going to find anything in the dark, anyway?" Mr. Seidman said, and he snapped on the overhead lights and Andrew turned his face away. "God, Andy, it looks like a tornado hit this place."

"I don't know what to do, Bob," Andrew said, "I just don't know what to do. I know I left it here."

"Now where did you leave it?" Mr. Seidman asked as he walked across the room.

"I—"

"Andy, what's wrong with your face?" Mr. Seidman asked quietly and with a seriousness Andrew had not heard before.

Andrew had almost no self-control left. "What's wrong

with my face! What's wrong with my face, Bob? Well, I have a slight skin condition. I've seen the dermatologist. It's a pesky little rash, but it doesn't burn too much. DO YOU HAVE ANY OTHER QUESTIONS?"

"All right, all right, calm down," Mr. Seidman told him. "Let's worry about that complaint. Is it on your computer?"

"It should be, but it's just not!" Andrew said. He punctuated the *not* by pounding on his desk.

"Let me try," Mr. Seidman said. "You know our system is programmed always to make a backup of any file that's worked on. It's gotta be here."

"It's not!" Andrew said.

"What's the file name?" Mr. Seidman asked. He stood at the computer keyboard and bent over to see the screen more clearly.

"H-L-one," Andrew said. "It should be under H-L-one, but it's not."

Mr. Seidman scanned several data directories and agreed that it wasn't there, at least under that name. "Let's try some other combinations," he said.

"Fine," Andrew said, "just fine." He was emptying the trash can onto the floor. "Wait!" he said. "Here's something!" He put one piece of paper aside and frantically examined the rest, then threw them to the floor angrily. "Just the cover page," he said. He did not take the time to wonder why the cover page would be in the wastebasket. "Try some combination of H-L-one point R-E-V," he said. "Try anything!"

"All right," Mr. Seidman said. "All right."

Andrew kicked around the papers on the floor, sometimes picking up one and then throwing it down again.

"It's not here, Andy, it's just not here," Mr. Seidman said. "Maybe you forgot and left it home?"

"Bob, I was here until two in the morn—"

"Some sort of problem?" asked a voice from the door, and Andrew and Mr. Seidman looked up to find Mr. Kenton in the doorway.

How the hell did he know? Andrew thought. "Yeah, Walter," he said, "some sort of major problem. Some moron lost the Highline complaint."

"Isn't that due in about fifteen minutes?"

"Yes, Walter, it is, and it's not here!" Andrew said.

"Then I would say that is a problem," Mr. Kenton said. "We'll have to beg for an exten—"

He was interrupted by yelling from the hall. "We found it!" Shelby yelled. She burst in, followed by Jamey and Rachel. "The whole thing, including the floppy disks, was—"

"Never mind that now! Where's the messenger?" Andrew said.

"He's outside," Jamey said.

"No, forget the messenger," Andrew said to Jamey. "You go! Now!"

Jamey looked surprised, but Mr. Seidman nodded, and Jamey rushed out.

"I thought you told me you were working on the hard disk," Mr. Seidman said.

"I was," Andrew said, "I was! I think," he added after a pause.

"You cut it a little close, didn't you, Andy?" Mr. Kenton asked, and before Andrew could answer, Mr. Kenton added, "I'd like to see you tomorrow morning."

Mr. Kenton walked out quickly, then Mr. Seidman, then Shelby. Rachel stayed behind and closed the door.

"Andy, what happened?" she asked.

Andrew sat at his desk, exhausted. Somehow, he had just made a big mistake: He had almost lost a major case for his firm, and his client, by default. He was too tired to answer Rachel, and he just shook his head.

"Never mind, don't worry about it now, Andy," Rachel told him. "We've got to get you out of here."

"Oh, God!" Andrew said. "I left Miguel at the hospital."

"And that's were you belong," Rachel said. "I'll walk out with you."

"What about this mess?" Andrew said. "I can't leave it like this."

"I'll take care of it. I'll get Shelby to give me a hand."

Andrew agreed; he was too tired to do anything. He walked to the door slowly, like an old man, and then stood by Rachel looking back at the mess for a few moments. Finally, he motioned Rachel out and shut off the overhead lights, leaving on the one on his desk. He shut the door and then walked to the main elevators, not trying to conceal anything, with Rachel beside him. People fell silent when they approached, staring. "Thanks," he said to Rachel as the doors opened.

"I'm going with you," she said. She held the door for Andrew.

"No, Rach, please. Help Shelby clean up my office. And tell her I'm sorry."

"You sure you don't need me?"

"I'm sure, Rach. Thanks."

"Okay," she agreed, and she gave Andrew a kiss on the cheek. When he was inside she took her hand away and the doors closed quickly and quietly, and then Andrew leaned against the wall and fought against tears, not completely succeeding in keeping them away. He did not want to go to the hospital, he just wanted to be at home with Miguel; he wanted to have his own things around him, he wanted to rest in their own bed with Miguel's arms around him. He needed that now, not the stark impersonal feel of the hospital. When he left the building, he hailed a cab and rested his head against the back of the seat, remembering earlier, happier times, times filled with joy, with sunshine, with love, and when the cab reached the hospital he told the driver to wait.

———

An hour later, Andrew was totally exhausted, too exhausted to talk, too exhausted to think, and he rode home from the hospital in the cab with his head on Miguel's shoulder. Within a minute or two he was fast asleep and Miguel had to wake him when they reached their building.

"C'mon, Drew, we're home," Miguel told him, shaking him gently.

Andrew opened his eyes and looked blankly at Miguel; for a few moments he did not recognize Miguel and he did not know where he was.

"Honey, it's me," Miguel said, and Andrew nodded, trying to mask his confusion, and then he remembered the previous few hours.

"Oh," he said, "we found the complaint."

"I know," Miguel said. "Are you going to get out of this cab?"

"Oh, sure," Andrew said. He was still not completely awake, but he opened the door carefully and stood outside while Miguel paid the fare, and when he got out Miguel said, "Are you all right, Drew?"

"I'm okay. I just couldn't wake up for a moment there."

"Do you think you should go back to the hospital?"

"I think I should go upstairs and go to bed," Andrew said. "Please."

"You're the boss," Miguel told him, and they went inside and while they rode up in the elevator Miguel held Andrew's hand so tightly that Andrew had to tell him it hurt.

"Oh God, this place is a mess," Andrew said when they were inside. He dropped his coat on a chair.

"And it's going to stay that way until you get into bed," Miguel told him. "Once I get you set I'll clean up."

The slight disorder in the apartment made Andrew uncomfortable, but he agreed; he was *very* tired. "Okay, just let me listen to the messages. I want to make sure everything went all right."

"I wish you'd forget your damned office!" Miguel told him. "It just doesn't matter. Only your getting better matters."

"Don't yell at a sick man," Andrew said as he pushed the buttons on the answering machine.

"I'm sorry, but you know I just want the best for you, and that office of yours is making you worse."

Andrew smiled. "I know."

There were a couple of messages from friends asking how Andrew was, and then there was one from Shelby: "Andy, Mr. Wheeler wants to see you in the executive conference room at nine-thirty tomorrow morning. I hope you're feeling better. Bye."

Andrew shut the machine off. "That can only mean trouble," he said.

"I hope you're not going to the office tomorrow," Miguel said.

"Miguel, I have to. I can't ignore a summons from Mr. Wheeler. I could get fired for doing something like that. Now I'm going up those stairs and getting into bed."

Miguel gave up about the office for now, because he knew how important work was to Andrew. He was not, however, ready to give up about Andrew's health. "Aren't you even going to eat some dinner?" he asked.

Andrew was partway up the winding metal staircase and he stopped and said, "After a day like today, would *you* want to eat anything?"

"You do have a point," Miguel said. "How about if I bring you some tea?"

Andrew really did not want tea, or anything else, but he told Miguel he would like some in order to make him happy, and he asked Miguel to call the friends who had left messages and tell them that he was all right. He climbed the rest of the way to the second floor of their triplex loft and undressed without turning on the light, which helped him not to see the lesions on his legs. From the windows he could see the soft winter dusk descend on the city. The tops of a few of the taller buildings still caught a bit of the sun, low in the sky in the southwest, and were colored a pale orange; below there was shadow, and in the streets between the tall buildings it was already very dark. For a moment Andrew forgot about everything and just watched the sunset until finally the last line of orange had faded away from the tallest building, and then he got into bed.

"Miguel," he called down.

"I'll be right up with your tea," Miguel called back.

"Never mind the tea for now," Andrew replied. "Just come up for a minute."

Miguel ran up the stairs. "What's wrong?" he said.

"Nothing, I just wanted to talk with you."

Miguel sat on the bed and combed Andrew's hair through his fingers. "So talk, baby. I'm listening."

"I'm going to take Dr. Gillman's advice and get a catheter. That way you can help me with the medications here at home. I just can't miss much more work, and this will mean I don't have to spend hours at Dr. Gillman's office."

"I do not want to talk about things like that," Miguel said, his Spanish accent becoming thicker. "I want you to stop going to your office and just worry about getting better."

"Miguel, you know I'm not going to get better. I'm doing okay, but this is about as good as it's going to get."

"Please do not talk like that. You are going to *beat* this! *We* are going to beat this!"

"Oh, Miguel, my friend, my buddy, I'm going to be here for a while."

Miguel rubbed his eyes. "You've got to beat this, you've just *got* to!"

"I'm trying, love."

Miguel turned away.

"You'll help me with the IVs?" Andrew asked.

"You know I will," Miguel said. "And right now I'm going to get you some tea." He kissed Andrew on the cheek and ran downstairs so Andrew could not see his tears.

Andrew slept badly. The lesions were bothering him, and then when he would wake up, trying not to scratch them, he worried about his meeting with Mr. Wheeler in the morning. He knew he was in for a good lecture, probably one of Mr. Wheeler's fatherly talks, something about how important this case was, how important his position at the firm was, and how important deadlines were. He did not think he was in any serious trouble because this was the first problem he'd had at the firm — everything else he had done had come out well, and he almost always won. That did not mean, however, that his conversation with Mr. Wheeler would not be unpleasant. The fact that the meeting was in the executive conference room instead of Mr. Wheeler's office meant that the meeting would be formal. Andrew was being called on the carpet.

Andrew spent the last hour of the night lying awake waiting for the alarm while Miguel slept peacefully beside him. Andrew could not avoid thinking about his meeting with Mr. Wheeler, but he also worried about his illness, and when he worried about that, he worried about Miguel, who, Andrew knew, was going to have to face life alone sooner or later. Miguel refused to talk about it, but Andrew knew that he thought about it. As Andrew lay awake, he watched the sky lighten and he waited for the day, and then suddenly the alarm buzzed. He had fallen asleep for a few minutes and he awoke exhausted. It required effort to shut off the alarm, and much more effort to actually get out of bed. Miguel barely stirred, and Andrew thought, lucky guy, and he kissed his lover's forehead lightly and headed for the shower.

The cold, harsh light of the bathroom showed Andrew his lesions more clearly than he wanted to see them, and he quickly got into the shower and turned the water on as hot as he could stand it. The room filled with steam, and he stood under it with his eyes closed, drifting, trying not to worry, remembering how nervous he had been on his first day of work at Wyant, Wheeler. His reveries, if that is what such a combination of old good memories overlaid with anxiety could be called, were interrupted when Miguel opened the door and said, "Drew, are you all right?"

"I'm fine," he said.

"You're not really going to work, are you?" Miguel asked.

"Yes, I told you I have to. I have a meeting with Mr. Wheeler at nine-thirty."

"I really wish you wouldn't go in, Drew," Miguel said.

Not this morning, Andrew thought, please. "Listen, Miguel, I'm only going in for half a day. Now you'd really be an angel if you'd shut the door—it's freezing in here—and make some coffee."

"You promise half a day?" Miguel asked.

"I promise," Andrew told him.

Andrew showered quickly and dried and got dressed while Miguel fussed downstairs in the kitchen. Andrew could smell things cooking and it made him feel sick to his stomach. When he went down there was one place set at the table, set with the good china and antique sterling flatware that had come from Miguel's family.

"My baby's going to eat," Miguel said, coming out of the kitchen with a platter holding eggs, sausages, English muffins, and some slices of fruit on one end. Andrew had to run into the bathroom when Miguel put the platter on the table.

It took more than an hour for Andrew to get Miguel calmed down, put on his makeup (an operation that Miguel refused to participate in), choose a tie, convince Miguel that he should teach his classes that day because he would definitely come home and get back into bed at lunchtime, and promise Miguel that yes, he would call him at the Institute if he needed help. Finally, Andrew was out of the building and in a cab. If he was lucky and traffic was light he would get to the office only a couple of minutes before his scheduled meeting. His stomach did not feel good.

He went in the main entrance this time, not sneaking in as he had the day before, and when he reached Wyant, Wheeler it was already past nine-thirty so he did not go to his office, but directly to the meeting. He realized as he walked through the halls that people were watching him carefully, sometimes whispering after he passed, and when he saw Rachel she called out, "Good luck." He was wondering what exactly he needed good luck for — this was, after all, just a session on the carpet and most of the other associates had had one at some time or other during their tenure at the firm. When Andrew reached the conference room, Mr. Wheeler, Mr. Kenton, Mr. Killcoyne, and Mr. Seidman were all there, arranged around one end of the table—and they were not smiling—and Mr. Wheeler's secretary was there to take notes.

Andrew stood at the door, stunned. This was going to be a major dressing-down.

"Come in, Andy," Mr. Seidman said. "Would you mind hitting the windows?" he asked, and Andrew closed the blinds. With only the harsh fluorescent lights glowing, the room looked like a death chamber.

"Thanks for coming in," Mr. Wheeler said.

"Of course," Andrew said. He could feel the seconds pass, one by one.

"Sit down, Andy, sit," Mr. Seidman said. Andrew took a seat diagonally opposite the partners. He still could not believe he was in this much trouble.

"Andrew," Mr. Wheeler said, "before we begin I'd like to say that everyone in this room is your friend."

"I know that, Charles," Andrew said. A few more seconds passed.

"More than your friend. Family," Mr. Wheeler said.

Right, Andrew thought. "Charles," he said, "I really apologize for the Highline mishap yesterday." He gave the group his best little-boy smile. "Those were a scary few minutes around here, but thank God the complaint was found and no damage was done."

"This time," Mr. Kenton said. "But what about *next* time?"

"There won't be a next time. I guarantee it." Andrew could hear his own heart now, feel it beating in his temples.

"Andy," Mr. Wheeler said, "it seems that something has come over you lately. A kind of stupor, a fogginess, a lack of focus. Earth to Andy," he said for emphasis. "Anybody home?"

"Hallooo," Mr. Kenton said sarcastically, waving his hand slowly in front of Andrew's face.

"That's right, Andy," Mr. Killcoyne said. "The last four or five months you've seemed really out of it."

"At least different, somehow," Mr. Seidman said, more gentle than the others.

Let's keep this positive, Andrew thought. "Perhaps you're right," he said. "I've certainly been busy with the Highline complaint, a preliminary injunction hearing, and the Microdex trial all falling at the same time."

"Some people think you have attitude problems, Beckett," Mr. Kenton said roughly.

The entire tone of the meeting had shifted suddenly; it was getting ugly. "And who thinks that, Sir?" Andrew asked.

"I do," Mr. Wheeler said.

I can't believe even Mr. Wheeler is against me, Andrew thought, shifting in his seat. "I had no idea there was a concern in that area," Andrew said. "Hey," he said, trying the smile again, "I'll get to work on it right away."

"Well, Andy, we've been talking it over," Mr. Wheeler said. "We think your future is, ah, we feel that, because we respect you so much we have to be honest with you."

"I'm all for honesty," Andrew said.

"Are you really, Beckett?" Mr. Kenton said.

"Yes, Walter, I am." Andrew stopped. Suddenly he understood. He had heard stories about Mr. Wheeler's little good-luck-and-get-out speech, always given in front of the other managing partners and always recorded by a secretary. Around the firm, it was called "The Executioner's Song," and Andrew realized that this was it. "Excuse me," he said, "am I being fired?" Only a second or two passed, but it felt like an eternity.

"Let's put it this way, Andy," Mr. Wheeler said. "Your place in the future of this firm is no longer secure. We don't think it's fair to keep you here where you're limited. But we do wish you luck, Andy, all the luck in the world."

Andrew suddenly felt sick; the kind of life he had enjoyed so much, and had always assumed would continue, was over in an instant.

Mr. Wheeler stood, gave Andrew his best paternalistic smile, and said, "And I hate to rush you out of here, but we've got a meeting in my office."

Everyone stood, smiling pleasantly, as though they had all enjoyed some trivial conversation, not destroyed a career.

"Excuse me, Charles," Andrew said. "With all due respect, this is preposterous. It doesn't make any sense—it sounds like we're talking about somebody else. Pardon the lack of humility, but I've had the distinct impression that I was one of the rising stars around here, and I'm sure that wasn't just my imagination. I think I deserve to know what is really going on around here!"

"Oh, you're right, Beckett," Mr. Kenton said sarcastically, "you don't have an attitude problem."

"Take it easy, Walter," Mr. Wheeler said.

"If you'd lost confidence in me, why did you give me the Highline case?"

"Andy!" Mr. Seidman said. "You nearly blew the case, for God's sake! That alone is inexcusable. It could have been catastrophic for us. Put yourself in our shoes, Andy."

"Bob!" Mr. Wheeler warned.

"There's no coming back from a mistake like that," Mr. Seidman continued, "regardless of who you are." He sounded sad about it, but he definitely supported the others. He paused a moment. "I'm sorry, Andy," he said softly.

"I see," Andrew said.

"Good luck, Andrew," Mr. Wheeler said, and one by one the partners and Mr. Wheeler's secretary left the room. Then a man walked in.

"Mr. Beckett?"

"Who are you?"

"I'm here to escort you to your office so you can organize your belongings."

In large law firms when an associate is fired he or she is immediately a pariah, and in the two hours it took Andrew to go through his office and pack his personal things—

unassembled moving boxes had already been thoughtfully placed in the hall outside his door by the time he got back from the meeting — only two people spoke with him: Shelby said she was sorry and started crying before she ran out, and Rachel came in and helped pack for a while, trying to make small talk. As she stacked picture frames in a moving box she finally asked, "So what are you going to do?"

"I don't know," Andrew said.

When Andrew was almost ready to leave, one more person came in: the office manager. She had done this many times before and she was all business. "Where would you like your things sent, Mr. Beckett?" she asked, and Andrew gave her his home address, which she wrote down carefully in a stenographer's notebook. "We'll have the boxes taken over this afternoon," she said. "Is there anything else?"

"Yeah," Andrew said, "can you get rid of this goon so I can have a minute or two to myself?" He nodded at the security guard, who had said almost nothing during the entire time Andrew was cleaning and packing, but who had watched carefully to see that Andrew did not pack anything that belonged to the firm or included client information. Andrew was not even allowed to take cards from his phone file, and there were a lot of personal numbers in it.

"I'm sorry, Mr. Beckett," the office manager said. "It's firm policy."

"I figured." Andrew took a last look at his office, the walls and desk now bare, and he felt as though it was not real, as though he was watching someone else from a distance, and he left with the security guard behind him. In the halls, people parted in front of him like the waters of the Red Sea parted for Moses, and no one spoke. The guard not only escorted him to the elevator but went down to the lobby with him and walked him outside. When Andrew was out of the building the guard said, "Good luck, Sir," and that was the end of Andrew's association with the prestigious law firm of Wyant, Wheeler, Hellerman, Tetlow, and Brown.

Miguel was already home by the time Andrew arrived. "What are you doing here so early?" Andrew said when he came in to find Miguel waxing the floor in the living room.

"I had somebody take my classes," Miguel said. "I wanted to make sure you really came home after your meeting. If you didn't I was going to call Rachel and come and get you."

Andrew dropped his coat onto a chair and went to the shelves holding CDs. Something big, he thought, and he first took out a Mahler symphony and then reconsidered and took out a Bruckner symphony and put it on and turned the volume up high.

"Uh oh, Bruckner," Miguel said, "something's wrong." Andrew usually played Bruckner when someone died, letting his emotions be swept along with the enormous expanse of the music.

"Yeah," Andrew said after a minute or two, "I got fired."

"Fired! They can't fire you!"

"Well, sweetheart, they did."

"All the hours you've worked for them! All those cases you've won!" Miguel's accent started to get very thick.

"I think I'm going to sue them." Andrew started quietly. "They know I'm the best associate they've got." He paused for a second. "I mean I was the best associate they had. Things haven't been the same since Mr. Kenton saw that lesion on my forehead. That's got to be why I was fired." The music rose with a brass choir ascending and Andrew's voice rose with it. "They cannot fire me for having AIDS! It's a simple matter of right and wrong. Of justice!"

Andrew looked into space then, seeing nothing, riding with the music.

———

The next morning after Miguel left for the Institute, which he did only after protest because he did not want Andrew to be alone, Andrew sat at the table with a cup of coffee and a long yellow legal pad and tried to assemble the outline of his case:

1. He was the best associate in the firm and a better lawyer than many of the partners. This

was not opinion, but could be verified simply by examining his record.

2. He was trusted with the Highline case, an immensely prestigious and potentially very lucrative case.

3. At the very time he was given responsibility for Highline, Mr. Kenton saw a lesion on his forehead.

4. Mr. Kenton knew what KS looked like because he had worked with Melissa Benedict, who had KS and who was open about having AIDS, and therefore he knew that Andrew had KS.

5. A couple of weeks later the Highline complaint disappears, although he was sure he had left a hard copy on his desk and copies of the files on his computer.

6. Mr. Seidman sees the lesions on his face.

7. The next morning he is fired. The excuse is the Highline complaint, which was probably sabotage, but the real reason is that the partners, or at least Mr. Kenton, did not want him around because he had AIDS.

He looked at his notes again and again, sometimes adding to them, sometimes turning to another page and making notes about conversations or other tiny incidents he remembered that he thought might be significant. The morning passed without him realizing it, and he had typed everything on his computer and was just printing it out when Miguel called to ask if Andrew wanted him to come home to make lunch.

"Lunch," Andrew said. "Who needs lunch? I'm on a roll — I've got them. I can't lose."

"First," Miguel said, "if you don't promise to eat some lunch, I'll be there in twenty minutes to see that you do. And second, how are you going to handle a case like this by yourself?"

"I will eat lunch, I promise. And I'm not going to handle this case by myself. There's an old saying that a lawyer who represents himself has a fool for a client. I'm no fool."

"We can discuss that some other time," Miguel said, laughing. "Now you *promise* you'll eat lunch?"

"I promise," Andrew said, "I promise."

"Okay, I trust you," Miguel told him, "I'll bring home something good for dinner."

It took Andrew another few minutes to get Miguel off the phone, and then, because he had promised that he would, he went to the kitchen to look for something to eat. Nothing looked appetizing at all, although there was a lot of food in the refrigerator. Finally he picked up a banana from the fruit bowl on the counter and took it back out to the table and got a telephone directory to try to pick a law firm. His first choice would have been Peterson, Lehigh, Monroe, and Smith, because they had an excellent litigation department, but unfortunately they sometimes represented either the firm of Wyant, Wheeler or individual partners, so bar association code on conflicts of interest ruled them out. The same was true for Andrew's second choice, but he was sure that it would be easy to find a firm to take the case. Wyant, Wheeler had the reputation of being, as one newspaper reporter had put it, a pack of Dobermans, and there were many attorneys who had been bruised who, Andrew was sure, would like a chance at revenge.

Andrew decided to start with Rodney Bailey's firm. Hopefully, he wouldn't get Bailey, but he was sure the firm would like the chance to get back at Wyant, Wheeler for the loss of the Highline case. Andrew made an appointment with one of the litigation partners, a Mr. McDermott, for ten the next morning.

Mr. McDermott was a large man who had worked very hard to overcome his Irish-immigrant background — his office was elegantly decorated, Abstract Expressionist paintings hung on the walls, and he was dressed immaculately, with a proper half inch of starched, snow-white cuffs showing beneath the sleeves of his custom-made dark blue suit. He knew Andrew by reputation, and he greeted him effusively; he assumed that Andrew wanted to talk to him about leaving Wyant, Wheeler for an early partnership with his firm, and it was something he was willing to consider seriously. Attorneys like Andrew Beckett were rare; they had an extra spark of brilliance, or intuition perhaps, that enabled them to see quickly and clearly through thickets of complexities that some lawyers would never understand and others would understand only through dogged persistence.

"Well, Mr. Beckett, I've certainly heard of you," Mr. McDermott said. He shook Andrew's hand and indicated a chair, then sat behind his desk. "What can I, and my firm"—he motioned around expansively—"do for you?"

"I want to sue Wyant, Wheeler for employment discrimination," Andrew said bluntly.

"You want what?!"

"They fired me yesterday because I have AIDS," Andrew said. "I have a good case."

All of Mr. McDermott's cordiality vanished. "You want to take on Wyant, Wheeler? You want *me* to take on Wyant, Wheeler?"

"That's right," Andrew said. "Standard fee arrangement, you keep one third of any award."

"Son, you don't have a chance," Mr. McDermott said, and there was nothing that Andrew could do to convince him otherwise. Within ten minutes Andrew was being shown out; Mr. McDermott did not shake Andrew's hand when he left, and as soon as Andrew was gone, Mr. McDermott went to the partners' bathroom and washed his hands for a full five minutes.

"You're going to take the skin off your hands," one of his partners told him.

"It's just some ink."

Over the next two weeks the scene was repeated day after day. As soon as a prospective attorney heard that Andrew had AIDS and that he wanted to sue Wyant, Wheeler for discrimination the conversation turned frosty and Andrew was rushed out as soon as the limits of decency allowed. And almost always the attorney washed his or her hands thoroughly as soon as Andrew left.

It was a disheartening time for Andrew. He missed the excitement of being in the office; he missed his former colleagues; he missed the intellectual challenges of the work; he missed the excitement of litigation, the little rush of adrenaline he got when he went in front of a judge; he missed consultations with clients. There was an unexpected financial dimension also: Because he had been fired he could not get disability payments, and because he had been fired "for cause" Wyant, Wheeler offered no severance pay at all. His last check, for two days' work, was sent to his home and that was the end of his contact with the firm, at least as far as the firm was concerned. It was difficult for Miguel, too. Andrew was home whenever he was not searching for an attorney—even the visits to Dr. Gillman's had been cut back because he had gotten a catheter implanted so he could take his medication at home — and because he was not used to sitting around doing nothing, he was in a terrible mood, which reached its peak one afternoon when he yelled at Miguel for over-cooking a piece of fish.

"Look, Drew," Miguel snapped back. "I can't believe we're fighting about food. You've got to pull yourself to-gether. Get a hobby or something."

"I'm a lawyer!" Andrew yelled. "I am not about to sit around and collect stamps or butterflies or something!" He pushed his chair out from the table and ran up the stairs and turned on the television just in time to see Joe Miller's commercial, the one that began: "If you or some-one you know has been injured through the fault of oth-ers, you may be entitled to a cash settlement for your pain and suffering." That's the one, Andrew thought, suddenly: He's black, so he understands discrimination, and he's not a bad lawyer, and I can help him with the rough spots. Andrew picked up the phone and dialed.

———

While Andrew was watching Joe Miller's commercial in the comfort of his home, two miles away, Joe's wife, Lisa, was under bright lights in a green-tiled delivery room giving birth to a baby girl, their first child. Mother and daughter were doing fine, but Joe was not. He was trying to get a camera to work while the newborn was still in

Lisa's arms, but he could not concentrate because he was so awed by it all, and besides, his hands were shaking. "Oh my God, a girl, oh my God. How do you load this film? Oh my God."

Lisa smiled. She loved her husband, clunker that he was sometimes. "Give me the camera, Joe," she said, and she took it and loaded the film and handed it back while a nurse grinned.

Joe took the entire roll of film in a matter of minutes, exclaiming "Oh my God," again and again.

"You'd think he'd done the work," Lisa told the nurse.

"Men!" the nurse said, laughing. "Why don't you go outside and get some air for a few minutes. I don't want you fainting on me."

"Why, I wouldn't —" Joe started.

"I've had bigger ones than you go down," the nurse said. "That floor's awfully hard."

"Go on, Joe," Lisa said. "Everything's fine."

"I'll be right outside," Joe said, and he rushed out, retrieved his portable phone, and called his secretary.

"Iris! It's a girl!"

"Congratulations! How big?"

"I don't know, Iris. Small, baby-sized."

"I mean how much does she weigh?"

"I don't know. Fifteen, twenty pounds. Listen, could you do me a favor?"

"Sure, Boss."

"Go to Famous Fourth Street Deli and buy a pound of Nova. No, she likes Scotch salmon better, get that. Oh heck, get a pound of both, and a dozen onion rolls, some bagels . . . Hold on."

A man was being rolled down the hall in a wheelchair, and Joe gave him a business card.

"Hey!" the guy said. "Joe Miller. The guy from TV. Thanks."

Joe flashed him a thumbs-up and said, "Give me a call," and went back to his telephone. "And get a bottle of Champagne — Dom Perignon."

"That's a hundred bucks a bottle, Joe. You sure?"

"A hundred dollars? Better get a good California instead. And get everything over here right away. She's starving."

"You got it, Boss," Iris said.

"Wait," Joe said. "Any calls I should know about?"

"The usual stuff. Nothing to worry about. There was one, though. Somebody named Andrew Beckett. Said you knew him. Wants an appointment."

"I never heard of any Andrew Beckett. But give him some time in a few days. And listen, pick up some chopped liver too."

Joe's offices were on the second floor of an old building in the downtown section of Philadelphia, and when

Andrew saw how run-down the area was and how tawdry the offices looked from the outside he did not go in immediately but crossed the street to watch what kind of people went in and came out. A whole family wearing neck braces went in, followed by someone who looked as though he was from the Caribbean, followed by someone on crutches. Andrew could see Joe standing near a window, obviously talking to someone. Andrew wished he could hear, but he could not.

"Mr. Findley," Joe was saying, "how big was this hole you fell into?"

"Four feet by four feet. Two and a half feet deep."

"And this hole was right in the middle of the street?"

"Right."

"Why didn't you cross at the crosswalk, Mr. Findley?"

"Why should I?"

"Explain this to me like I'm a six-year-old, Mr. Findley, okay? The entire street is clear except for one small area under construction, with a huge hole that is clearly marked and blocked off, and you decide you *must* cross the street at exactly this spot. You fall into the hole, and you want to sue the city for negligence?"

"Yes. Do I have a case?"

"Yeah. Yeah, sure you have a case. I want you to go with my assistant, Iris, and fill out some forms. She'll tell you about our fee arrangement. Of course you know we don't get any cash unless we get cash justice for you. By the way, how's your back since the accident? Any dizziness, nightmares?"

"Now that you mention it . . . "

As Joe showed Mr. Findley to the door he moved out of Andrew's range of vision and for a moment Andrew was unsure whether he would actually go in or not. It's my last chance, if he won't take the case, no one in Philadelphia will, he thought. Then he crossed the street and climbed the creaky wooden staircase to the second floor. This certainly isn't Wyant, Wheeler, he mused, as he gave his name to the receptionist and was told to take a seat.

He sat in the bare waiting room waiting for Mr. Miller — he had specified that he wanted to talk to no one else — while another attorney was using the room to interview a potential client, the man from the Caribbean Andrew had seen going in.

"How's it going?" the attorney asked.

"How's it going? I need an immigration lawyer."

A man across from Andrew stared fixedly at Andrew's face, which looked worse than it had when he had been fired.

"But MacReady and Shilts are not immigration lawyers," the lawyer told the potential client.

The man staring at Andrew got up and got a magazine from the rack beside the old-fashioned coat tree.

"But I saw the commercial of Joe Miller — for pain and suffering. I have pain and suffering from the Immigration Department."

The man returned to his seat and continued to stare, not looking at the magazine.

"No," the lawyer said, "that means pain and suffering from accidents."

The man was still staring. Andrew made a face at him, and the man quickly looked down at the magazine.

Iris came to the door and said, "Mr. Beckett?"

Andrew stood.

"This way, please." Iris led Andrew to Joe's office, and when she announced his appointment, Joe said, "Come in, come in."

"Good to see you, Counselor," Andrew said. He shook Joe's hand. "Remember me? Judge Tate, Kendell Construction?"

"I do!" Joe said. "Limestone! Innocuous! How are you?" He led Andrew inside, then looked at Andrew more closely and said, "What happened to your face?"

"I have AIDS."

"Whoa-oh!" Joe stepped back. "Sorry, I . . ."

"It's okay," Andrew said. "May I sit down?"

"Uh, yeah." Joe went behind his desk and Andrew sat directly in front of it, and took off his hat, which revealed a large, ugly lesion on his forehead.

Andrew looked around the office before he spoke again; it was old and dusty, although fairly neat. The firm's name was painted across the windows. Joe himself was thin and handsome and Andrew thought that Joe looked as though he could have fit in at a firm like Wyant, Wheeler and he wondered why Joe was practicing what is often considered the lowest form of law: personal injury litigation.

There was a box of cheap cigars on the desk, and Andrew wondered if there had been a new arrival in Joe's family. He did not look like the cigar type.

"New baby?" Andrew asked.

"Yeah, a little baby girl."

Andrew picked up a cigar and read the wrapper. "Oh yeah, 'It's a girl.' Congratulations."

"One week old," Joe said.

"Kids are great!" Andrew said.

"Thanks, Beckett. I'm real excited about it." Joe glanced at his watch. "What can I do for you?"

"I was fired from Wyant, Wheeler. I plan to bring a wrongful discrimination suit against Charles Wheeler and his partners."

"You want to sue Wyant, Wheeler, Hellerman, Tetlow, and Brown?"

"Correct," Andrew said. "I'm seeking representation."

Jesus, Joe thought, how can I get this guy out of my office? "Continue," he said.

"I misplaced an important complaint. That's their story. Want to hear mine?"

"How many lawyers did you call before you called me?" Joe asked.

"Nine."

"That's not exactly a vote of confidence, is it?" Joe said. "But continue."

"I was diagnosed with AIDS about eight months ago, during a bout of pneumonia. I recovered quickly and went back to work in ten days. I was doing so well on my medication that we decided against telling anyone about it, except friends, of course."

"We?" Joe asked.

"My lover and I."

"Your *lover* and you?"

"Miguel Alvarez. He's from Spain. He teaches at the Institute of the Arts. He's also an amazing painter."

"Yeah? My wife paints now and then. She's good, I think, but what do I know? Anyway, continue."

Andrew noticed that there was a small patterned weaving on the wall that looked southwestern, and he wondered if Joe's wife had made it. "After the pneumonia," he said, "I dove back into work. Everything was fine until the KS showed up."

"KS?"

"Kaposi's sarcoma. It's the AIDS-related skin cancer that causes these lesions." Andrew pointed to his forehead.

"I see," Joe said, and he could see the lesions very plainly. "Continue."

"First I had them on my legs, then my forearm, then my back, then my face. When they hit my face, I worked at home for a while waiting for the chemo to kick in."

"So how'd you get fired?"

"They say I lost a very important complaint, but I *know* I left it there. And not only did the complaint itself vanish, but even my computer files were gone. And then it was mysteriously found at the last minute. And the next thing I know, the following morning I'm being escorted by a security guard to pick up my belongings."

"So you were concealing your illness?" Joe asked.

"Correct," Andrew said. This is not going well, he thought, not at all.

"Okay, explain this to me like I'm a two-year-old," Joe said, "because there's an element I can't get through my thick head. Didn't you have an obligation to inform your employers you had this dreaded, deadly, infectious disease?"

"No! I did not! And besides, that's not the point! From the day they hired me to the day they fired me, I served my clients consistently, thoroughly, and with absolute excellence. And if they hadn't fired me, I'd still be doing that today!"

"Okay, okay, calm down." Joe thought for a minute or two. "So you're saying they didn't want to fire you for having AIDS so, despite your *brilliance*, they tried to make you look bad. Hence, the mysterious lost file. Is that about it?"

"It was a complaint. I was sabotaged. And yes, that's about it."

"I don't buy it, Counselor —"

"That's very disappointing," Andrew interjected.

"— And I don't see a case." Joe took out a pack of Rolaids; this was not going to be a good day.

"I do have a case!" Andrew said. "If you don't want to take it for personal reasons —"

"Thank you, Counselor, I don't," Joe said firmly.

There went Andrew's last hope. "Thank you for your time, Counselor," he said, and he stood and went to the door.

"Beckett?"

"Yes?"

"I'm sorry about what happened to you. It's a bitch."

"Don't send flowers, my friend. I'm not dead yet," Andrew said, and he left with dignity, not showing his disappointment, not showing his exhaustion. "Have a nice day, Mr. Beckett," Iris said as he walked out, and he nodded, remembering what George Burns said about that phrase: Every day I'm above ground is a nice day.

Joe's associate Filko watched Andrew leave. "What the hell's wrong with that guy?" he said.

Iris shrugged as Joe came to her desk. "Iris, find out if Dr. Armbruster can see me," Joe told her.

"Armbruster? When?"

"Today sometime. Soon! Right away!" Joe said, and he went back to his office.

"And what the hell's wrong with *him*?" Filko said.

Dr. Armbruster had been treating Joe since he was a child. When he had graduated from medical school, black physicians were something of a rarity, and of those few, many went into research or teaching, fields where they would not have to worry about building a practice. But not Dr. Armbruster: He went back to his neighborhood and opened a small family practice and as his patients prospered, so did he, until he finally allowed himself the luxury of a nice house on the outskirts of the city. A few years later, he moved his practice into part of his house, and not only did many of his old patients come to his new offices, but new patients came from his new neighborhood. He was proof of the maxim that through hard work comes success. He also knew Joe very well, and he could see that Joe was upset.

"Come in," he said, "come in." He asked about Lisa and the new baby and Joe's law practice and then finally, when Joe was settled down a little, he asked, "So why are you here, Joe?"

"Well, I know this sounds silly, like I'm overreacting, but there was this man with AIDS in my office and I shook his hand and with the new baby and everything . . . "

"So you had contact with someone with AIDS and you're worried," Dr. Armbruster said, and he took out a blood pressure cuff.

"I'm not worried," Joe said. "And what are you doing?"

"I'm going to take your blood pressure. Roll up your sleeve. And relax!"

"Yeah, sure, okay," Joe said. "I didn't have contact anyway. What do you consider contact? I mean, we were sitting in the same room, three or four feet apart. What about shaking hands? No, I know, of course you can't get it by shaking hands, you've got to be sharing needles or something, right?"

"Right, and would you please be quiet for a minute." Dr. Armbruster pumped up the cuff and watched the dial. Joe was upset. "The HIV virus can only be transmitted through the exchange of bodily fluids." The doctor went to a cabinet and Joe stood and paced.

"Yeah," Joe said, "but isn't it true, Doc, that they got all kinds of new things that they've found out about this disease? You tell me now that there's no danger, I go home, I pick up my little baby girl, then I find out six months from now, oops, we made a mistake. You *can* get it from clothes, skin . . . What're you doing!"

Dr. Armbruster had brought out a needle and some plastic tubes. "We're going to draw some blood," he said.

"Exactly why are *we* going to do that?"

"Joe, I don't care a whit about your private life, but—"

"Doc! You're going to give *me* an AIDS test? That guy was just sitting in my office, Doc. You said yourself you can't get it that way! It doesn't travel through the air. You can't get it by breathing or touching, right?"

"Not by touching, not by shaking hands, not by hugging, not by using the same toilet. Even kissing someone with AIDS is safe. But if there's something in your past that you're worried about, let's find out."

"Listen, Doc, I don't need an AIDS test," Joe said, and he rolled down his sleeve, put on his coat, and started to leave. "What do you mean, in my past?" he asked from the door.

"Joe, come back in, and shut that door."

Joe came back a little way into the room.

"IV drug use?" Dr. Armbruster asked.

Joe shook his head.

"A homosexual encounter?"

"Yo, Doc! This is me you're talking to."

"Unprotected sex with a prostitute?"

Joe thought about this one for a moment. "Not really."

"Unprotected sex with anyone you didn't know very well, any time within the last twelve years?"

Joe put his coat down and rolled up his sleeve.

Joe had always prided himself on not being sexist. He did his share of chores around the house. He got up in the night with the baby as much as Lisa did, always helped with the cooking, and that night he put on an apron and helped Lisa make dinner. He thought about Andrew's visit and he watched his wife work; she was small and thin and very pretty, and he thought about how lucky he was.

"Why are you so quiet, honey?" she asked.

"Just thinking about the day," Joe said, and then he told her about Andrew's visit to his office, although he did not tell her about visiting Dr. Armbruster.

"You've always had this thing about gays," Lisa told him.

"No, I don't," Joe said.

"Yes, you do. How many gays do you know?"

None if I can help it, Joe thought. He busied himself with the salad for a moment and then said, "How many do *you* know?"

"Lots," Lisa said.

"Like who?"

"Karen Berman, Aunt Teresa, my cousin Tommy, who lives in Rochester, Eddie Mayers from the office, Stanley, the guy who's going to put in our kitchen cabinets."

"Your Aunt Teresa is gay!" Joe said. He stopped working on the salad. "That beautiful, sensuous, voluptuous woman is, is, a, *lesbian*!" Joe had trouble with the word, and the thought was even worse.

"That's right," Lisa said.

"Since when?" Joe demanded.

"Probably since she was born," Lisa said. "Come on, let's bring this stuff into the dining room."

"All right, I admit it, I'm prejudiced," Joe said, following Lisa and carrying the salad. "I don't want to work with a homosexual. You've got me."

"Okay, Joe. Get some napkins, will you."

That's it? Get some napkins, Joe thought. She's going to give up that easily? "I mean," he said, "two guys doing that thing together. Can't you see it? 'Is that yours?' 'Is that mine?' I mean, I don't want to be in bed with anyone stronger than me or who has more hair on their chest than I do; it's a rule I live by."

Joe was trying to be funny, but Lisa frowned and looked away.

"Hey, call me old-fashioned, call me conservative. I think maybe you have to be a man to get just how disgusting the whole damned idea is."

Lisa gave Joe a little hug to show that she wasn't really angry. "My little caveman," she said.

"You're damned skippy," Joe said.

Throughout it all, the baby, firmly strapped into her infant seat on the table, smiled, and Joe went to her and stroked her face gently.

"You stay away from your Aunt Teresa," Joe told the baby.

"Don't say that," Lisa told him.

"And another thing!" Joe said. "The way they work

out, pumping up so they can be macho and faggot at the same time. I can't stand that shit. Now I'm being totally honest with you."

"That is perfectly obvious, Joe. Now are you going to sit down and eat?"

The disapproval in Lisa's voice made Joe uncomfortable, and he tried one more time. "Would you take a client if you were constantly thinking, 'I hope this guy doesn't touch me! I hope this guy doesn't even *breathe* on me!'?"

"Not if I were you, honey."

Four

Joe had forgotten about Andrew Beckett; his HIV test had come back negative, his practice was busy, his daughter growing by the day. He was thinking about getting his wife some little gift — maybe the special scarf she wanted, although why anyone wanted a scarf that cost more than $100 he didn't know — when he stopped into the deli for a pastrami sandwich to take to the library with him. When he came out, instead of dropping money into a panhandler's hat, he handed him a business card and breezed on.

God, he thought, he wished his law firm had a decent library. Law libraries are very costly to maintain, however, and like most small practitioners, he kept some essential reference books in his office and used the public law library, maintained by the bar association, for more detailed research. At least this library was nicer than most, with its

Windsor-style armchairs and two sets of green-shaded reading lamps on each table, and the staff was always helpful. Joe found the books he needed, then he picked up some others—for their size, not their content—that he piled around him on the table so no one could see his sandwich. He started reading. God, he thought, what I wouldn't give for someone to do this grunt work for me. He worked steadily for a half hour or so, occasionally taking a bite of his sandwich, or hiding it when the security guard ambled by. He was not thinking about anything but his work when he heard a chair scrape especially loudly across the floor. When he looked up, he saw Andrew Beckett taking a seat at a table across the room. "Shit," Joe muttered, and he piled all his books in front of him and ducked down behind them. Joe thought Andrew looked terrible. He was unshaven and wearing a bandanna on his head, and he was coughing. Joe wondered what was wrong with him now.

With Andrew's immune system permanently out to lunch, he was a candidate for an entire textbook of exotic diseases, but the thing that was making him the most uncomfortable was a common, ordinary cold. His eyes were running, his nose was dripping, and his throat was sore; as he had told Miguel that morning, he felt like hell. Nevertheless, as he had also told Miguel, fool for a client or not, since he could not get anyone to represent him, not even anyone from Philadelphia's horde of personal injury lawyers, he was going to represent himself, and particularly in this case time was of the essence. Cases like this could drag on for years, and Andrew did not have years, which is why he was in the library, cold or no cold.

Andrew opened his briefcase and took out a legal-size file folder, a yellow legal pad, a pen, and tissues. He placed them neatly on the table in front of him and then went for a book. When he came back, it was obvious he was going to be there for a while. The woman at the other end of the table glared at him every time he coughed or sneezed and finally picked up her books and papers and moved. Andrew did not notice; he did not even notice when a librarian came over with a book.

"Sir?"

Andrew didn't look up.

"Sir, this is the supplement you were looking for."

Andrew looked up and smiled.

"You're right," the librarian said, "there is a section on"—the librarian lowered his voice—"HIV-related discrimination."

"Thank you," Andrew said. "Thank you very much."

"We have a private research room available," the librarian told him.

"I'm fine, thanks," Andrew said. He coughed and looked in his briefcase for more tissues.

"Wouldn't you be more comfortable in a private room?"

"No," Andrew said. Then he realized what the problem

was. "Would it make you more comfortable?" What an ugly sweater, Andrew thought; the librarian was wearing a baggy black sweater with a large diamond design in white. It would have looked great on a fit young man, but the librarian was neither.

Before the librarian could answer, Joe came over. He tried to make it casual, but stress showed in his voice. "Hey, Beckett," he said, "how're you doing?"

"Counselor!" Andrew said, surprised. "Oh, fine, I think."

The librarian gave up and moved away, shrugging to another patron as if to say he had done all he could.

"So, who'd you get?" Joe asked.

"What?"

"Who'd you get? Did you find a lawyer?"

"Oh," Andrew said. "I'm a lawyer. How's your baby?"

"What?" Joe said. He actually wanted to talk about Andrew's case. It was kind of a test for him, to prove that he wasn't as homophobic as his wife had said. Besides, just talking couldn't do any harm, could it?

"Your baby," Andrew said. "Remember?"

"Oh, great. She's doing great."

"What's her name?"

"Lorice."

"Lorice. That's a beautiful name."

"Thanks. I named her after my sister," Joe said.

Andrew nodded and went back to his work, and Joe

stepped back as casually as he could and watched for a minute and then came back. "So how did they find out you have AIDS?"

Andrew was tired of talking about this, but he was also polite, so he answered. "One of the partners spotted a lesion on my forehead."

"Right," Joe said. He sat down across from Andrew. "Explain to me, how do you get from one lawyer spotting a lesion, which could have been anything, to the partners deducing that you had AIDS, and then terminating you based on that conclusion?"

"Good point," Andrew said, and it *was* a good point; it was the logic upon which the case depended. He took a legal pad out of the file folder on which he had made notes about that very issue. "The partner who spotted the lesion, Walter Kenton, used to work for Walsh, Almer, and Brahm in DC. There's a paralegal there, Melissa Benedict, who's had lesions on and off for three years. She says it was common knowledge around the office that she had AIDS, which caused the lesions."

"They didn't fire her?" Joe wondered how Andrew knew about Melissa, but he did not ask.

"No, they didn't."

"So this Kenton connected your lesion and whatever suspicions he had about your personal life with this woman who had AIDS, and he blew the whistle on you. Suddenly files are missing—"

"Not files, a very important complaint."

" — So suddenly a very important complaint is missing and it's time to let you go, literally overnight. But, you've been their Golden Boy, their rising star. It's like two plus two equals three. You're right, their behavior is inconsistent."

"Thank you," Andrew said, and he meant it; at least someone agreed with him. He had been feeling as though he had stepped through the looking glass, but now he felt a little better about the possibilities of his case.

"Got a relevant precedent?" Joe asked.

"The Arline decision."

"Arline?"

"Supreme Court." Andrew pushed the report across the table toward Joe, who looked at Andrew's hand, then at the book, and after a pause, he turned the book around and began reading.

" 'The Federal Vocational Rehabilitation Act of 1973 prohibits discrimination against otherwise qualified handicapped persons who are able to perform the duties required by their employment . . .' " Joe looked up at Andrew. "Maybe you really do have a case," he said.

"Thank you," Andrew said again.

Joe continued reading. " ' . . . Although the ruling in *Irwin* did not address the specific issue of HIV and AIDS discrimination — ' "

Andrew finished the quote from memory. " ' — Subsequent decisions have held that AIDS is protected as a handicap under law not only because of the physical limitations it imposes, but also because the prejudice surrounding AIDS exacts a social death which precedes the actual physical one.' "

Andrew stopped and looked at Joe, staring into his eyes without flinching. It was a test, a challenge.

After a moment Joe turned back to the book. " 'This is the essence of discrimination: formulating opinions about others not based on their individual merits but, rather, on their membership in a group with assumed characteristics. . . . ' "

They were both quiet. God, I hate this case, Joe thought, but the guy is right. Still they did not speak, then Andrew sneezed loudly.

"Bless you," Joe said.

There are many perquisites for a senior partner in a major law firm in addition to being treated like a deity by one's staff. The senior partners at Wyant, Wheeler had even more fringe benefits than their counterparts at similar firms. There were memberships in all of Philadelphia's best private clubs, membership in a club in Palm Beach and two in New York, "business meetings" in exotic tropical locales, and of course there were season tickets to all major cultural and sports events. All of these extras classified for tax purposes as business expenses and were justified, with the exception of the "business meetings" (in February it is so much more pleasant to conduct business in St. Thomas or Fiji than in Philadelphia), by the assertion that these expenses were necessary for entertaining clients. Actually, that was not completely untrue. Sometimes important clients were taken to a posh club or to the symphony or a baseball or basketball game, but mostly these perks were enjoyed by Charles Wheeler and his senior partners. Of all the perks available to Mr. Wheeler, the one he enjoyed most was not the symphony or the clubs, but the private box in Spectrum Arena. The owners of the boxes were allowed to decorate them as they pleased, and Mr. Wheeler had spared his firm no expense, with costly prints on the wall, a small kitchen, a bar, comfortable furniture, and a television monitor in case someone actually wanted to follow what was happening in the arena. One night, shortly after Joe and Andrew met in the library, Mr. Wheeler and his senior partners and all their wives, along with an important client and his wife, were enjoying the Seventy-Sixers while Mr. Wheeler waited for the little surprise he had planned, which happened right on schedule: As everyone except Mr. Wheeler was watching the game, Julius Erving walked into the box and clapped him on the shoulder.

"Hi, Charles."

"Julius Erving!" Mr. Wheeler announced. "Come in and say hello to my friends."

Erving, dressed in an elegant dark suit with a perfectly tied bow tie, was greeting everyone in his easygoing and gracious manner when Joe Miller arrived.

"Charles Wheeler?" Joe interrupted.

"Come in!" Mr. Wheeler said. He did not know who Joe was, but because he was black he assumed he was a friend of Dr. J's.

"Got a summons for you," Joe said to Mr. Wheeler, handing him an envelope. "Dr. J!" Joe said. "Nice to meet you. Let me give you my card in case you ever slip and fall." He handed Dr. J. his business card and turned to the group before closing the door. "Enjoy the game!"

There was a startled silence. "That was the guy from TV," Dr. J. said. "Say, Charles, what's happening?"

"I don't know, but I sure as hell am going to find out," Mr. Wheeler said. He opened the summons and read it. "That son of a bitch!" he muttered. "How *dare* he!"

"Come on," he ordered, "we're going to the office." He did not address anyone specifically, but Mr. Seidman, Mr. Kenton, and Mr. Killcoyne all got up. No one else moved.

"Come on!" Mr. Wheeler ordered again, and he walked out, followed by the others.

Mr. Wheeler did not wait to get to the office. He was angry, *enraged*, that someone would actually name him, Charles Wheeler, in a lawsuit, and not only that, but that he was served with papers in front of the wives, and, worse than that, a *client*. He began issuing instructions as soon as they left the box.

"Interview every employee, every associate, every partner! Did *any* of them know Andy was sick? *How* did they know? Did he tell them? Did they notice something wrong with his appearance? Why didn't this information get to the managing partners? Why were we left in the dark?"

"Charles," Mr. Seidman started, but Mr. Wheeler ignored him.

"Regarding Andy: I want to know everything about that little pervert's personal life. Did he frequent those pathetic bars on Chestnut Street?"

"Jesus," Mr. Seidman said, but Mr. Wheeler continued to ignore him.

"—And what about other homosexual facilities, whatever disgusting things they might be."

"Charles," Mr. Seidman said again, and again he was ignored.

"—And what deviant groups or organizations did he secretly belong to?" He stopped as Mr. Seidman grabbed his arm. "What is it, Bob?" he snapped.

"Let's make a fair settlement offer and put this whole tragic mess behind us," Mr. Seidman said.

Mr. Wheeler stopped and faced Mr. Seidman. "Look, Bob, Andy brought AIDS into our offices, into our men's rooms, he brought it to our annual goddamn family picnic!"

"We ought to be suing him," Mr. Kenton said angrily.

What is Kenton's problem? Mr. Seidman thought. He tried to insert some rationality into the conversation. "For Christ's sake, Walt, where's your compassion?" he asked.

"Compassion! Beckett sucks cock, Bob. He takes it up the ass. He's a goddamned pervert!"

Mr. Seidman was astonished at Mr. Kenton's hatred. "That's kind of extreme," he said. "Andy's private life is none of our business."

"Bob," Mr. Wheeler said, "you are trying my patience. Andrew Beckett is making his private life our business. We gave him Highline. Did he say, 'I'm sick. I might not be able to see this through'?"

"He was doing a great job," Mr. Seidman said.

"Bob," Mr. Wheeler said, "I must ask you to shut the fuck up. Did Andrew Beckett say, 'I might not be able to serve our clients to the best of my ability'? No. He said nothing. He discarded the trust and affection I bestowed on him —"

Getting a little regal, aren't you, Mr. Seidman thought, but he said nothing.

"—And now Andrew Beckett proposes to haul *me* into a court of law, to sling accusations at me, to call me a *bigot* in full view of the Philadelphia judicial establishment."

"Beckett doesn't want to go to court," Mr. Killcoyne said. "He's hoping for a quick, tasty settlement."

"A jury might decide he has a case," Mr. Seidman said thoughtfully.

"Wait just one minute," Mr. Wheeler said. "The man was fired for incompetence, not because he had AIDS. You didn't know he was sick, did you, Bob?"

"Holy shit!" Mr. Kenton said quickly, *too* quickly, Mr. Seidman thought. "Did you, Bob?"

Mr. Seidman considered his answer carefully. "No. Not really," he said.

Mr. Wheeler shook his head in disgust and walked away, followed by everyone except Mr. Seidman, who watched them for a moment, thinking. He had a very bad feeling about this, as if something was going to go terribly wrong.

———

Joe Miller did not particularly like Andrew Beckett and he did not particularly like Andrew's case, but Joe did believe in the law, and he thought that Andrew deserved representation; he could say truthfully that he took Andrew's case for the principle, not the money. Discrimination law, however, was an area he had never considered until then. He was sure there was money in it, and one morning two weeks later he was thinking about his new television commercial and planning copy for a new sign.

"Iris, where's my coffee?" he demanded as he came in. "Filko, how was the vacation?"

Every law firm has one attorney like Filko: young but aging fast; hardworking, taking the worst assignments without complaint; steady; dependable; and totally without imagination.

"Charles fucking Wheeler?" Filko said. "Are you crazy?"

"You heard," Joe said.

"Here's the coffee," Iris said, putting down his mug in front of him.

"It's the local branch of the ACLU," another colleague said to Filko.

"You're a Republican, Joe!" Filko said.

"So what?"

"You belong to the NRA!"

"And I'm a damned good shot," Joe said. "Tell me, Filko, how many toilet stalls are there in the women's rest room on this floor?"

"How many *what*?"

"Two," Joe said. "I checked. And how many toilet stalls are there in the men's room? Two, *plus* four urinals. Now, Filko, how many wheelchair-accessible toilets are there in either of those rest rooms?"

Filko thought his boss needed a vacation.

A phone rang and Iris reached for it.

"Zero!" Joe said. "How many in this entire building? Zero! Get the picture, Filko? That's discrimination."

"It's Wyant, Wheeler's attorney," Iris said. "They're asking for a postponement on the pretrial."

"I'll call them back," Joe said. "I've got to talk to my client.

"Those low-life sleazy sons of bitches," he said to Filko. "Of course they want a postponement."

"Charles fucking Wheeler," Filko said.

"They're asking for a postponement when I've got a

client with a terminal disease! They're going to drag their damned heels every step of the way."

"Joe, you're crazy," Filko said.

"Get me Beckett," Joe said to Iris.

"Listen, Filko," Joe told him, "you find yourself a qualified, female, paraplegic legal assistant, or lawyer, who is qualified to work here, except that she can't take a leak because there's no wheelchair-accessible toilets and there are more toilets in the men's room anyway, and you've got yourself a sex discrimination suit and a disability discrimination suit. Double the revenue!"

Joe went into his office, leaving Filko to think it over.

Andrew was holding when Joe picked up the phone. "Hey, Beckett," he said, "this is Miller."

"What's up?" Andrew said.

Joe could hear opera in the background—some woman wailing about something. "Listen," he said, "those sons of bitches want a postponement."

"Yeah?"

"Well, I just wanted to know what you thought."

"Your call, Counselor," Andrew said.

"Okay," Joe said. "I'll rattle their chains a little and try to speed things up. Hang in there."

"I will, Counselor," Andrew said. "Thanks."

They said good-bye, and then Miguel called down from the bedroom, "Who was that?"

"My attorney. Wyant, Wheeler wants a postponement. I think they're hoping they can outlast me."

Miguel's response was unintelligible, and Andrew laughed a little. Mornings were definitely not Miguel's best time of the day.

One of the disheartening unpredictabilities of AIDS is that sometimes, after a week or two of general malaise, when one is too tired to do much more than sleep, but even sleep comes badly, there will be a time when suddenly you wake up one morning and feel great: hungry, ready for the world, maybe even tingling a little. The disheartening part of this is that the remission, if that is what it is, can go away as quickly and unexpectedly as it came.

This was one of those good times for Andrew. He had already cleaned the kitchen and living room thoroughly — something that he would not have had the energy to do a week earlier — and now he decided to make a real breakfast. "Coffee's brewing, and breakfast is in thirty minutes!" he called up to Miguel. "Rise and shine!"

"Christ," Miguel said, too low for Andrew to hear. "Okay, dear."

Andrew had a very good day. He cleaned some more, shopped, and then spent most of the rest of the day reading Joyce; he intended to get through *Ulysses* once more, and now that he was not working he had the time to do it. It is easy to get lost in the meandering complexities of Joyce's writing, and when Andrew was next conscious of the hours that had passed, he had missed the time he set aside every day for his "meditation," as he called it.

Their loft had a large living area on the main floor, bedrooms above it along a balcony that overlooked the living room, and another large room above the bedroom level where Miguel painted and Andrew escaped. Andrew put down his book and climbed the two flights of stairs to the studio and made himself comfortable. He closed his eyes and just listened to his own breathing for a few minutes, and then turned on a tape recorder. He sat in a corner against the windows. The studio had two entire walls of windows and nearly fifty tropical plants. Warmed by the late-afternoon sun, Andrew closed his eyes and repeated the mantra after the woman on the tape.

"I can heal myself," the voice said.

"I can heal myself," Andrew repeated.

"I can heal myself."

"I can heal myself."

The litany went on for some time, and then the sound of the sea came up, accompanied by gentle, formless, futuristic music, and the woman's voice said, "Think of yourself floating through the air, floating through the upper atmosphere, able to touch down wherever you desire —"

Andrew tried to make himself feel lighter, to float; he listened to his breath and as he became conscious of it, it slowed, and he did feel lighter.

" — Imagine yourself floating over islands, islands in a tropical sea, warmed by the sun's healing rays — "

Andrew tried to see a tropical island from a distance high above, and when he did he saw Miguel, tanned, running along a beach on an island in the Mediterranean. The water was the purest turquoise, and a gleaming white yacht passed offshore, and Andrew was running behind him, strong, healthy, ignorant of the virus that was already inhabiting his body, and then when he thought about the virus the tranquil feeling was lost.

" — Embrace the healing powers of the sun. Embrace the warmth of the sun. Feel the sun's energy wrapping itself around you — "

How Miguel did love the sun, Andrew thought, not the sun in Philadelphia, but the sun in remote, sea-touched places —

" — Feel the sun's energy wrapping itself around you, encircling you, strengthening you, and say, 'I can heal myself.' "

"I can heal myself," Andrew repeated.

"I can heal myself."

"I can heal myself." Andrew thought again of Miguel running along a beach, and he felt terribly sad.

"I can heal myself."

"I *can* heal myself," Andrew repeated, and then he heard the door open downstairs and Miguel come in. He did not want to disturb the tranquillity just yet so he repeated over and over, quietly, "I can heal myself," as he heard Miguel climbing the stairs.

"Drew, you listening to the quack again?" Miguel said when he came to the top of the stairs, and the mood was broken.

"Who knows what will work?" Andrew said.

"If you ask me, she's just found a way to make lots of money off other people's misery," Miguel said.

"I can heal—"

Andrew shut off the tape.

"Miguel," he said gently, "it makes me feel better."

"And that makes *me* feel better," Miguel said, "but I still don't like her."

They spent a quiet evening together. Andrew put on a favorite recording of *Madame Butterfly* and settled into a comfortable chair with his copy of *Ulysses*, and Miguel sat across from him, sometimes looking at Andrew with great affection, filling page after page in a sketch pad with quick, clean, sure drawings. Finally, Butterfly came to her heart-wrenching end, beautifully sung by a young Renata Scotto, and Andrew was suddenly, terribly tired.

"I've had it," he said. "I'm for bed."

"Me too," Miguel said, and they shut off the lights and climbed the stairs together. When they were in bed, Andrew rested his head on Miguel's chest for a minute and Miguel held him.

"I was coming out of the gym today, and I ran into Jimmy Paisler," Miguel said. "Remember him?"

"Nasty queen with muscles," Andrew said.

"That's the one. Do you know what he said to me? He looked at me all weird and tragic-like and said, 'What's it like, knowing your boyfriend's going to die?'"

"Thanks a lot, Jim," Andrew said. "Of course, he never has had a boyfriend for more than a week or two at a time."

"I wanted to kill him!" Miguel said.

"So what did you say?"

"I said, 'You know, Jimmy, everyone's going to die, but my lover is not going to die of AIDS. There's going to be a cure, and he's going to be around to take advantage of it!'"

"You still believe it, don't you?"

"Yes," Miguel said firmly, "and it will be something simple, like one injection, and people with AIDS will become healthy again."

Andrew moved to his own pillow and rubbed Miguel's cheek with the back of his hand. "I love you," he said.

"I love you too."

———

Wyant, Wheeler's defense strategy was in three parts: Overwhelm, intimidate, and finally, if it got that far, use an extremely good litigator for the courtroom. They hired Philadelphia's other major law firm as their counsel, and the overwhelm part started within days of the evening Joe had served papers on Mr. Wheeler. The firm assigned five lawyers to the case, and they immediately started burying Joe's office in paper: a motion to dismiss, motions for discovery, motions on every tiny piece of civil procedure that had the remotest possibility of being relevant. The intimidation was also carefully planned. Everyone on the team was instructed to remind Joe continually that he was dealing with a large, prestigious firm. The attorneys were instructed not to make calls to Joe's office themselves, but always to have a secretary call and ask if Joe would hold for whomever from Peterson, Lehigh, Monroe, and Smith, and when Joe did speak with one of the opposing team that person was as cold as he or she could be without passing the bounds of professionalism. It made things even worse for Andrew that the judge assigned to the case was an old-line moneyed patrician whose opinions about most things matched those of Charles Wheeler.

Their tactics did not work: Joe was the wrong person to try to intimidate, and one morning when he was in court responding to yet another nuisance motion he told the judge very plainly that although he believed in trying cases in court, not in the press, this time he was going to expose the entire "corrupt"—Joe's word—legal establishment. The case had not yet hit the press, and the judge wanted to keep it that way. He ordered a settlement conference in his chambers the following week, and he ordered that all the principals be there.

The morning of the conference was cold and grim. The previous two weeks had been hard on Andrew, and he was tired, run-down, and he was taking some new medication that was making him feel ill. On top of it all, the morning of the conference he had to argue with Miguel to get him to agree not to go. By the time Andrew met Joe outside the courthouse, he felt as though he had been without sleep for days, and he looked haggard.

"Now listen," Joe told Andrew as they climbed the steps, "just let me do the talking. I want that mouth buttoned."

"You're the boss, Counselor," Andrew said, "but remember, any settlement has to include exoneration."

"I thought we hadn't agreed on that," Joe said.

"You hadn't. I won't sign any agreement that—" Andrew broke off, because coming down the corridor toward them was an entire phalanx of lawyers, including Mr. Wheeler, Mr. Kenton, and Mr. Killcoyne and all of their representatives. They were discussing strategy and did not notice Joe and Andrew at first, but then Mr. Wheeler saw them and stopped. "Good to see you, Andy. You're looking well."

Andrew knew he looked terrible. "Thank you, Charles," he said. There would be no "Mr. Wheeler" from Andrew.

The Wyant, Wheeler team filled the entire elevator, and

Joe and Andrew watched as the doors closed. "Jesus," Joe said.

"Big time," Andrew replied. "It's called 'we've got more lawyers than you do.' "

"Sounds like something we used to do on the playground when I was a kid," Joe said as they entered the next elevator.

"Do not underestimate these people," Andrew told him.

"Hey, Beckett, don't underestimate me."

Andrew thought that Joe did not have much of a chance against his competition, but he said nothing more, and they walked to Judge Garnett's chambers in silence. When they got there, Andrew sized up the competition, and it was formidable: an entire team, each attorney as good as the other. Joe would get very little past them even with his help, Andrew thought, and the judge they had ended up with made matters even worse, because he was from Mr. Wheeler's circle.

Judge Garnett had been a patrician Philadelphia lawyer with the right political connections. He had advised presidents, donated heavily to the Republican party, arranged thousand-dollar-a-plate fund-raising dinners, and his reward was his appointment to the bench. He was not an outstanding judge — he was not interested in the fine points of jurisprudence, and he had a reputation for being tough on drugs and soft on white-collar crime — but he was, for the most part, a decent and fair judge. Some attorneys thought his insistence on proper decorum occasionally verged on the fanatic, but there had been few complaints about him since he had been on the bench. He knew this and wanted his good record to continue. He did not want to see this case come to trial.

He looked at all the lawyers gathered in his chambers, seated in a rough semicircle in front of him. He smiled at Mr. Wheeler, and he said, "Let's begin. Attorney for the plaintiff?"

"Joseph Miller, Your Honor. MacReady and Shilts Legal Services."

"Yes," Judge Garnett said. "I've seen your television commercials. 'If you or anyone you know has been injured through the fault of others,' and so on. It should say 'through the *negligence* of others.'"

"Thank you, Your Honor. I'll take that under consideration," Joe said.

Not good, Andrew thought.

"On behalf of the defendants?" Judge Garnett asked.

"Belinda Conine, of Peterson, Lehigh, Monroe, and Smith."

"And Jerome Green."

"Ralph Peterson."

"Dexter Smith."

Even Joe, who was normally not very concerned about his opposition, was a bit intimidated. In addition to Ms. Conine, two of the firm's senior partners were going to participate in the litigation. Plus, Jerome Green was something of a legend in Philadelphia and a rarity anywhere:

a litigation partner of a major corporate law firm who was black. Joe wondered if they had picked him because of his color. He leaned toward Andrew to whisper something, but before he could, Judge Garnett said to him, "You're outnumbered four to one.

"Whom do I address?" he asked the others. "I can't talk to four lawyers at once."

"I'm chief litigant, Your Honor," Ms. Conine said. She was the third prong of Wyant, Wheeler's strategy: overwhelm, intimidate, and use Ms. Conine. She was a pretty, demure woman, but she was a ruthless strategist, often using her own soft-spoken femininity as a weapon. Even though her reputation was well known, again and again opposing counsel had underestimated her, to their immense detriment. As Mr. Wheeler had once said when she was on the opposite side of an issue, she could smile at you, then stick a knife in you, then ask you sweetly if it hurt, then call an ambulance. She was, Andrew thought with reluctant admiration for the choice, the perfect defense counsel for this case. She would have just the right combination of sympathy and steel.

Judge Garnett was quiet for a minute, looking carefully at each person in the room. He wanted to make certain that he had their attention. "I've taken the unusual step of asking the litigants to be present for this conference in the hope we can settle this matter today, among *ourselves*."

He looked at Joe, and Joe knew he was referring to his threat of the press.

"There is nothing I hate more," the judge continued, "than seeing two lawyers sue each other. If you look at the opinion polls, when Mr. John Q. Citizen is asked to rank professions according to the respect he holds for them, where are the lawyers? Somewhere below personal fitness trainers and only slightly above child pornographers."

Mr. Wheeler allowed himself a small smile. He had heard this speech before over Scotch at the club.

" — If we keep suing each other, if we fail to settle the smallest difference among ourselves with mutual respect, if we continue to scrap like bucks in heat — " He smiled benevolently at Ms. Conine, letting her know that, for the moment, she was one of the guys, and Ms. Conine smiled back sweetly. " — We will fall lower on that list. And when people lose respect for lawyers, they lose respect for the law. And when this society loses all respect for the law, we'll be murdered in our beds, my friends, our cherished institutions will be burned to the ground, and our children and grandchildren will live like savages."

Definitely the wrong judge for this case, Andrew thought.

"If it please Your Honor," Joe said, "we *hope* to settle this matter."

"By God, you *will* settle it!" Judge Garnett said, slapping his hand on his desk for emphasis. "If you force this case to trial, young man, you'll regret it for the rest of your natural-born days. Now, Joseph." He paused significantly and then continued, emphasizing every word.

"What would you require to settle this matter today?"

Everyone in the room sat up a little straighter or leaned forward a little: The next few minutes would decide the course of several lives for the next few months.

Joe spoke quietly, nonaggressively. "Reinstatement at full salary, back pay covering the period of unemployment, and—"

"Hold it, Joe," Judge Garnett said.

"He wants to come back to work, Chuck," the judge said to Mr. Wheeler.

Mr. Wheeler shook his head, as though he was disgusted. "That's impossible, Your Honor," Mr. Wheeler said.

"That's impossible, Joe," Judge Garnett said.

"Excuse me," Ms. Conine said, and everyone turned toward her. "If it please Your Honor, we are prepared to offer a cash settlement of twenty-five thousand dollars."

Joe shook his head. "Your generosity overwhelms me, Belinda, considering my client was earning over a hundred thousand dollars a year when he was terminated by your client."

"Give me a break, Joe," Judge Garnett said. "Let's cut through the false attitudes. Give them a figure. Now how much do you want?"

"*I* want to go back to work, Your Honor," Andrew said. He was so tired.

"You weren't listening," Judge Garnett told him, as if he were talking to a child. "Give me a figure, Joe."

Joe thought for a minute. "Based on what my client would have earned over the next three years, including benefits and projected raises, and the extraordinary cost of medical care for someone with AIDS, we would settle today for the very fair amount of four hundred fifty thousand dollars." Andrew immediately whispered into Joe's ear as the judge began to speak.

"Very good," he said. "Now, Belinda, I've got a figure over here of four hundred fifty. I —"

"One more thing, Your Honor —" Joe interrupted, and then Andrew interrupted him: "Any settlement agreement *must* include, and this is critical, a letter of exoneration, making it clear my termination had nothing to do with the quality of my work."

"Your Honor," Ms. Conine said sweetly, but very firmly, "Mr. Beckett's incompetence almost sabotaged a three-hundred-fifty-million-dollar suit."

"I was the one who was sabotaged!" Andrew said.

Ms. Conine ignored him. "We have complaints about Beckett's lack of preparation, his disorganization, his arrogant, defensive manner. The list goes on, and on, and on. We —"

"Hold on, Ms. Conine," Judge Garnett interrupted. "Chuck, what's the big deal? The boy wants a letter, to show his mother, for her to keep after he's gone. Why are you being so hard-assed about this?"

Mr. Wheeler spoke directly to Andrew. "I wish I could exonerate you, Andy, but I'd have to lie to do it."

This is it, Andrew thought, we go to trial. "You can save it for the courtroom, Charles," he said very quietly and very slowly. "I want to hear you say, under oath, in front of a judge and a jury, that I'm a bad lawyer."

Andrew got up and prepared to leave. "Your Honor," he said, nodding, and he took his coat from the rack.

"Don't do this, Andy," Mr. Wheeler said; it was almost a threat.

Joe walked to the door with Andrew. "What do you want them to say?" he whispered. "That you're Perry Mason?"

Mr. Kenton finally joined the proceedings. "A trial takes *time*, Andy. Do you know what I'm saying?"

"I think I catch your subtle drift, Walter," Andrew said.

Joe had been supporting settlement until that moment, but nobody was going to push around a terminally ill client of his—gay, straight, black, white, whatever—with a threat like that. "With all due respect, Your Honor, my client chooses to pursue his constitutionally guaranteed right to a trial. See you in court."

Joe and Andrew left together, and there was silence in the room. Mr. Kenton was turning red; Mr. Wheeler was more sad than angry, but he was worried.

"Hey, Lucas," Mr. Wheeler said to the judge, "how about lunch at the club?"

"Sure, Chuck. How are the grandkids?"

Five

J oe Miller called Andrew the morning after the settlement conference. "Now look, Beckett," he said, "I want you to consider this very carefully. Wyant, Wheeler has agreed to our figure of four hundred fifty thousand dollars, but that's it: no letter of exoneration, no nothing. Their position is that you fucked up. Period."

"Then I will not settle," Andrew said. "Tell me," he added, "does that mean you'll withdraw from the case?"

"No, Beckett, what do you think I am? But listen to me—let me tell it to you like you're a five-year-old, okay? They're going to make it very tough. They've had investigators looking into your past, and they've found stuff."

"What stuff?" Andrew asked.

"I don't know, exactly," Joe said. "Stuff about your 'lifestyle' and old 'tricks' I guess you call them."

"But that's irrelevant to this case."

"Yeah, sure, but that Conine woman is going to crucify you on the stand. Can you take that?"

Andrew thought about this. He could take anything, but what about Miguel? He was sure to be drawn into it, and his family was too. "Listen," he said, "my parents' anniversary is tomorrow and we're going down. I want to talk to them about this."

"I don't even know if I can keep the offer open to Monday," Joe said. "They wanted an answer today."

"If they want an answer today, the answer is no," Andrew said.

Jesus, Joe thought, I have a fee of $150,000 in the bag, and my *client* won't take the settlement. "I'll tell them that," he said. "They don't want to go to trial either, so it should be okay."

"Thanks, Joe," Andrew said. "You know," he added, "you're doing a great job."

"Yeah, great," Joe said, "talk to you Monday," and he hung up.

Miguel tended to get excited quickly, and he got very excited very quickly when Andrew told him about Joe's conversation. "They're going to give you a hard time? I'll give them a hard time!"

"Miguel, stop it. I've got a headache."

"Sorry, Drew," Miguel said, but he was breathing hard and he was wrinkling his forehead — always a sign of trouble.

Andrew rubbed Miguel's back lightly. "Listen," he said,

"things may come out about me that you won't like. They might even try to find out stuff about you."

"About me, there is nothing to find," Miguel said, and it was true. After he had fallen in love with Andrew there had never been anyone else, and there were only very few before Andrew. "And there is nothing about you that I don't like." Miguel paused for a second or two. "Even things I don't know, I like," he added.

Andrew really did have a bad headache from all the tension. He was sure the tension was probably hurting his overall health, too. "All right," he said, "we'll talk to my family tomorrow. It's time for my meditation," he said, and he thought, Boy, do I need it.

"Okay," Miguel said, "you meditate. Maybe it will help you get better."

Andrew climbed the two flights of stairs to the room with the windows and soon Miguel heard "I can heal myself. I can heal myself . . ." He took out a sketch pad and a broad, soft pencil and drew in a fury, filling page after page with thick, black, rough lines.

They arrived at Andrew's family's home early the next afternoon after passing through a brief snowstorm on the way. It was a modest house in a working-class suburb, situated on the front of a tiny plot, matched up and down the street by similar homes with similar white porches and brick steps on similar plots occupied by people from similar backgrounds. Most of the neighbors knew Andrew and Miguel, and if they had had any misgivings about their relationship, they had lost them long ago. Before Andrew got sick he and Miguel could always be counted on to help when a couple of extra sets of muscles were needed to move some furniture, and everyone liked Miguel—he had even painted portraits for several of the neighborhood families as gifts.

Miguel's parents had never visited Pennsylvania, and on this trip out to the suburbs Miguel had brought a video camera to take films to send to his parents. As soon as they got out of the car, Miguel began acting like a bad parody of a film director, pointing where he wanted Andrew to go and giving instructions in a loud voice. "Show us the house, Drew," he said. "And don't forget to talk into the camera." Miguel was even wearing a baseball cap like some young Hollywood hotshot.

"All right, everybody, this is my home," Andrew said obediently. "This is the house where I grew up, in my hometown, Lower Merion, Pennsylvania." He led the camera to a birdbath and bent over and brushed away the snow on the base, revealing several sets of child's hand prints embossed in the concrete. "See this, these are my cute little handprints, and my brothers' and my sister's." Andrew pointed to the prints and then straightened up.

"Good. And today is?" Miguel prompted from behind the camera.

"Today is my parents' fortieth wedding anniversary—El grande ruby."

"That's it," Miguel said from behind the camera, "the big ruby."

"And this is my neighborhood." Andrew waved, and the camera panned around.

"It must have been tough," Miguel's voice said, "living in this neighborhood, surrounded by poverty."

"Yeah," Andrew said on camera, "there are some mean streets out there." He went up the steps, across the porch. "And this is the front door. I caught a finger in this door once, this one here." He held a finger close to the lens. "Broke it too." He stepped inside, followed by Miguel and the camera. "This is the hallway. My mother calls it a foyer." The camera panned again as Miguel entered the house. A group of children chased each other through the hallway, screaming, a background of conversation could be heard from the kitchen, and then a pretty six-year-old girl raced in and screamed, "Uncle Andrew!" and jumped into his arms.

"This is my niece, Alexis," Andrew said to the camera. "You look so pretty. Say hello to the camera." But Alexis ignored the camera and blurted out, "Mommy's pregnant again!"

"You heard it here first, folks. That's great, another baby!" Andrew's sister came in, and Andrew smiled at her. She was thin, with short, well-kept blond hair, and Andrew thought that she looked great. He put Alexis down and Jill gave him a big hug.

"Hello, darlin'," she said, and Andrew turned her to

face the camera. "This is my sister, Jill," he said, "the most fertile woman on the planet."

Jill ran her hands across the tops of Andrew's shoulders. "You feel thin," she said. She noticed how short Andrew's hair was and wondered about it, but she did not mention it. "Miguel, put down that camera," she told him, and when Miguel handed the camera to Andrew she gave Miguel a big hug too.

"Hi, sweetheart," Miguel said. "Congratulations."

"Thanks, you handsome devil," she said, and Miguel certainly was handsome—both men's and women's heads turned when he walked down the street. "Is he eating?" she asked about Andrew.

"We do not discuss his weight," he told Jill. "Do we?" he said to Andrew. It was a sensitive topic between them, one that they sometimes argued about. Miguel had been determined that Andrew would not lose weight, but in spite of everything he could do—all the great cooking, desserts with calories that practically flew off the plate and stuck to him, the coaxing, pleading, yelling—Andrew had lost more than twenty pounds in the past nine months.

"Hey," Andrew said, "you know I'll eat well here. And speaking of eating, let's see who's in the kitchen." Andrew moved forward, panning with the camera as he walked into the kitchen, which was filled with women, several wearing corsages. In the Beckett family, special days—anniversaries, birthdays, holidays—were *important*. "Hi, Mom," Andrew said. "How do you feel on your fortieth anniversary? This is my mother, Sarah," he said for the benefit of the camera.

Andrew's mother was a pretty woman, well-dressed, and down-to-earth. Over the forty years of her marriage she had worked hard and had raised a happy, successful family, and now she was at the point where she could enjoy herself. She was so proud of Andrew, her lawyer son, and Miguel, her artist son, and her affection was obvious just from the expression on her face.

"How do you think I feel?" she said, laughing. "I feel invaded. Now put that camera down and give me a hug."

Andrew intended to give the camera back to Miguel, but one of Andrew's young nieces held out her hands and Andrew smiled and handed it to her. "Happy anniversary, Mom," he said with great tenderness, and he embraced his mother tightly.

"Thanks, Angel," Sarah said. She released herself and stepped back to look at him. "How are you feeling today?"

"Today's a good day," Andrew said.

"Oh good," Sarah said.

"Where's Dad?"

"He's out in the shed, trying to get the snowblower started."

Andrew turned back toward the camera. "It snows more than an inch for the first time in seven years, and Dad's out with the snowblower. Come on, Miguel, let's go find him."

They left the kitchen by the back door, and as soon as they were gone, Sarah relaxed and the worry showed in her face. Then she saw that the camera was still focussed on her and she said, "Put that thing down before the batteries run out."

Andrew's family had always been close. When Andrew was young, holidays had always included aunts and uncles from both sides of the family, along with all their children — Andrew's cousins. As the cousins grew up, celebrations began to include the cousins' spouses and eventually *their* children, and although Andrew's parents' house was not the largest in the family, all the major holidays were celebrated there. As the family grew, entertaining became a lot of work, and as his parents' fortieth anniversary approached, Andrew, backed by his brothers and sister, had suggested that his parents might like their children to give them a party in a restaurant or a club somewhere. It would all be the same, Andrew had promised, everyone would be there; the only difference would be that someone else would be doing the work.

Both of his parents had vetoed the idea without more than a few seconds' consideration. "I like having everyone here," his mother said, "and besides, if we went out there wouldn't be any leftovers to send home with people." "Foolish waste of money," his father said. That was the end of the discussion.

The party went well. There was enough food to feed three times the number of people, there was alcohol for those who wanted it—Andrew's family was mostly a non-drinking one—and, although the house was crowded, everyone found space somewhere. It would be wishful thinking to suggest that everyone was as comfortable with Andrew and Miguel as Andrew's immediate family was, but everyone was polite. There was some whispering about Andrew's health, but none of it reached Andrew or Miguel, and they both enjoyed themselves.

After everyone had eaten every bite they possibly could and after Sarah's large collection of commemorative plates was admired once again and the new flowered curtains that she had made were appropriately praised, space was cleared in the living room for dancing, and everyone from the very young to the old was included. Toward the end of what had become a clear, cold, starlit winter evening, as Andrew was dancing slowly with his mother and Jill was dancing with their father, Andrew's brother Matt said to Miguel, "Can you imagine two people being together for forty years?" "Yes, I can," Miguel answered.

Andrew had said earlier that there had to be a short family conference after everyone else had left—"This time he's going to tell us he's straight," Matt had joked—and sometime after nine that evening the immediate family gathered in the den: Andrew's father, Bud, with his American flag pin in his lapel; his mother; Jill and her husband, Jim, who did not want to be there; Matt and his wife; and his brother Randy and his wife. Andrew was holding Matt and Molly's four-month-old baby girl, and before he said anything he looked around the room, with its aging red Oriental rug that had once been a major expenditure for his family and had been the location of so many accidents and spills over the years, and he remembered previous family conferences. Perhaps the most significant had been when he introduced Miguel to his family. It was rough going, particularly with Andrew's father, but Miguel had brought a portrait of Andrew as a gift, which Andrew's father truly admired, and within a year everyone was very close.

Andrew started this meeting by jokingly taking attendance, but then he became very serious. They had known about his being fired from his job, but he had not told them that he was going to sue. He explained a bit about what was happening legally and what it was likely that the trial would be like, but he did not tell them much about Joe, deciding it was probably better not to shock them too much at once.

Finally he got to the point of the meeting. "There will be things said at the trial that may not be easy for you to hear. Things about my private life, maybe things I've done in the past. And there will be publicity, I'm sure." Andrew stopped for a moment. "I want to make sure it's okay with everybody here before I go forward."

"Do you want me to take the baby?" Matt's wife asked.

"No, she's fine," Andrew said, and he looked down and smiled.

His brother Randy sat closest, and Andrew looked to him first. Randy was the youngest, and he was the emotional one in the family; Andrew expected his support. "I appreciate you asking," Randy said, "but really, it's your call."

"Thanks, bro," Andrew said. "What about you, Jill?"

"It's fine with me," Jill said, "but, Andy, to be honest, I'm really worried about Mommy and Daddy. They've had to go through so much already, and now it's possible that —" Jill had to stop; she still found it hard to believe that Andrew might not be with them for much longer.

"Go on," Andrew said.

Jill wiped her eyes. "It's possible that there are going to be some hard times ahead. I wonder if it's fair to put them through this too."

That was precisely what Andrew was concerned about. Was it fair to put everyone through a messy trial *and* the stress his illness was sure to produce, and then a funeral? "Mom?" he asked.

Sarah was the strong one; the one who had held the family together through various crises over the years. If she said that she had had enough, there would be no trial: Andrew would take the offered settlement and go on permanent vacation.

"All I know is," Sarah said, and this was very difficult for her because she knew what was certain to come in the not too distant future, "you got through your diagnosis fine, like a trouper. But then when they fired you, you were so devastated. I don't expect any of my kids to have to sit in the back of the bus; we've worked too hard for that. Go ahead, fight for your rights."

"Thanks, Mom," Andrew said. "Dad?"

Bud was a large, balding, retired blue-collar worker. Life had not been easy for him. He had worked hard to provide well for his family and give his children opportunities that he had not had, and when Andrew had finally told him that he was gay it had crushed him. Bud had taken it as a personal failure, and he had been bitter and disappointed. Gradually, however, his love for his son overcame everything else. Bud was not comfortable talking about his feelings, however, and he certainly was not comfortable talking about Andrew's being gay. After all the time he had known about Andrew, after all the good times he had had with Miguel, Bud had never really discussed the topic, even with the family. And now, his son was going to push them all into the public eye. Bud said nothing at all for two or three minutes and the tension was so strong it created a physical presence in the room. When Bud did speak, it was very slowly and quietly. "Supposedly, the Lord doesn't give you more trouble than you can handle, but I'm having a hard time believing that these days."

Again, there was silence. Randy furtively wiped his eyes and Jill squeezed her husband's hand hard. Everyone knew that if Bud said to stop, Andrew would.

Andrew's father faced him directly, with tears in his eyes; although everyone could hear them, his words were for Andrew, no one else. "Andy, your mother and I always taught you to be proud, to fight for what you believe in. Well, things didn't turn out the way we planned, but, Andy, the way you've faced this whole thing, you and Miguel, with so much courage, your mother and I have been so impressed."

Bud had to stop to regain control of his voice and to think of exactly what he wanted to say. In those moments Andrew loved his father more than he ever had in his life.

"Andy," Bud continued, "I can't imagine there is anything that anyone could say that would make us feel anything but incredibly proud of you."

Everyone was quiet again, but now everyone knew that things would be okay.

"Thanks, Dad," Andrew finally said. "I love you guys. How about you, Matt?"

Matt was the blue-collar worker in the present generation, and it had taken him years to become comfortable with Andrew's being gay, but in recent years he had been a vocal supporter, following the struggle for gay civil rights in the newspapers, arguing with his buddies until even they were starting to change their minds about "faggots."

"Hey, you're my brother," Matt said. "That's all that matters! What are those bastards going to say about you? That you're gay? Hell, I knew that before you did."

"Wait a minute!" Miguel said, and everyone waited to see what the problem was. "Andy, you're *gay*?"

It was, everyone said, the mildest winter in years. If there was precipitation it was more often rain than snow, and Andrew's father had no more opportunities to use his snowblower. Andrew and Joe worked on Andrew's case from time to time, but as with all litigation, after a motion paper was filed there were many weeks of waiting before there was any more action. The rains of the winter continued into spring and after several more aborted settlement attempts it began to seem certain that the case would come to trial, and as spring passed into summer Andrew helped Joe prepare lists of witnesses and helped Joe with the responses to the never-ending motions brought by Wyant, Wheeler's attorneys.

Summer was beautiful, clear and dry and not too hot, and Andrew and Miguel spent as much time at the beach as they could. Andrew's KS seemed to be in remission, and his health was generally good, at least as good as it could be while having AIDS. He tired easily and, because of the damage that the sun does to the immune system, whenever Andrew went outside, he wore loose-fitting clothes that covered most of his body and he wore a large, floppy-brimmed white hat. But he and Miguel were happy; it was probably the best summer they had had together.

During the summer, Andrew did not spend much time working on his case, but Joe was working hard. Before a case like this comes to trial, both sides have the right to discovery, which is basically a chance to interview each other's witnesses under oath with the other side present and also to obtain copies of relevant documents. Because the range of material and topics allowed in discovery is much broader than the range of evidence admissable in a trial, one of the purposes of discovery is to ensure that there are no tremendous surprises for either side at the trial and to ensure that both sides know in advance what is going to be relevant, thereby preserving the Court's time and resources. As Joe worked on discovery throughout the summer, he realized that the trial was going to be a no-holds-barred nasty fight, and without ever telling Andrew exactly that, he tried to prepare him for it.

Andrew's health started to deteriorate at the end of August, and at the same time Wyant, Wheeler's attorneys tried every delaying tactic they could, so Joe started calling press conferences, explaining to the public that Wyant, Wheeler was not interested in the truth coming out, they were only interested in delaying the trial until his client was too ill to participate, or worse. What is it Wyant, Wheeler wants to hide so badly? Joe wondered aloud on the six o'clock news. This comment precipitated an angry telephone call from Charles Wheeler to his attorneys, who held a press conference the next day saying that the great firm of Wyant, Wheeler had nothing at all to hide, and in the interests of justice and out of concern for Andrew Beckett's health they would join with Joe Miller in petitioning the court for an immediate trial.

Andrew felt worse and worse; he was losing his hair from the chemotherapy, he had lost more weight and was constantly running fevers that Dr. Gillman could find no cause for. Even Joe was concerned, and he did his best to speed things up even more. It took only a day to empanel a jury, something of a record in such an important case, and Andrew thought they hadn't done too badly. There was an ex-Marine that could be trouble, but there was at least one likely lesbian and a young New Age man, and no one empaneled had looked at Andrew with obvious revulsion or disgust. Nevertheless, the day of jury selection was exhausting for Andrew, and when he and Joe left the courtroom, Joe told him to go home and get right in bed; opening arguments were the next day and he wanted Andrew rested and alert so he could take notes about things that might be relevant later.

Andrew did go to bed almost immediately, but sleep did not come for hours. Even after Miguel was sleeping peacefully beside him, Andrew was awake, looking at the dim lights visible through the windows, listening to the faint city sounds, worrying. He probably got four or five hours of sleep altogether, and then it was time to get up and prepare for the first real day in court. He dressed carefully, wearing a suit and a new shirt and tie Miguel had bought him for the occasion. He was thankful that the lesions on his face had faded so he did not have to use makeup.

Andrew had told his family and Miguel that it was not

necessary for them to be there, but everyone ignored him. "Those bastards are going to be there in force," Matt said, "and so are we."

It was an old courtroom, with mahogany panelling on the jury box and judge's platform and with old oil portraits of long-dead judges on the walls, and although Andrew had been in it and many similar courtrooms over the past six years he still felt a wave of anxiety when he entered. Everyone was in place at exactly nine o'clock. Joe and Andrew sat at one table, and Belinda Conine and an entire battalion of other attorneys sat at the other, along with the senior partners from Wyant, Wheeler. Mr. Wheeler sat in the middle, dressed in a splendidly tailored custom-made dark suit, and the rest of the Wyant, Wheeler partners were dressed almost as well. It was part of the defense strategy to make the partners appear rock solid, practically as trustworthy as God.

Andrew's family was there—his father wore a jacket over a black sweater for the occasion—as well as some of his friends, and of course Miguel. There was also a large contingent of associates and staff from Wyant, Wheeler. Although the Wyant, Wheeler staff was there to help the defense if necessary, they were all rooting for Andrew.

Everyone rose as directed when Judge Garnett came in and then listened attentively as he gave them his standard this-is-a-courtroom-not-a-circus speech, which included the instructions that the attorneys were to remain seated at their tables and speak into their microphones unless they were given permission to do otherwise, and then he was ready and all the work of the previous months came together and Andrew felt terribly ill, this time from nervousness, not from his disease.

"Mr. Miller, you may deliver your opening remarks while standing before the jury if you wish, or from counsel's table."

"I'll stand, Your Honor," Joe said, and he walked casually to the jurors' box, almost as though he were not even thinking of the impending trial.

Joe spoke quietly and slowly; no Perry Mason histrionics for him. "Ladies and gentlemen of the jury, forget everything you've seen on television and in the movies. There won't be any last-minute surprise witnesses. No one will break down on the stand with a tearful confession. You are presented with a simple fact: Andrew Beckett was fired. You will hear two explanations for why he was fired. Ours—" Joe looked at Andrew, then at Andrew's family and Miguel and the jurors looked too. "—And theirs." Joe looked at the army of lawyers on the defense side and the jurors looked in that direction; one of them nodded gravely.

"You will hear testimony about a certain 'missing' file. Don't be misled; this is not 'The Case of the Vanishing File.' This case is about something far more important than that. It's up to you to sift through layer after layer of 'truth' and determine for yourselves the version that is most true—"

As in all trials, Andrew thought. Andrew's father whispered something to Matt. Miguel listened intently. Charles Wheeler studied the patterns on the ceiling.

"—There are certain points that I must prove to you. Point number one—" Joe held up a finger. "—Andrew Beckett was, *is*, a great lawyer, a brilliant lawyer."

Mr. Wheeler's head came down, and he whispered something to Ms. Conine.

"Point number two—" Another finger went up. "Andrew Beckett, afflicted with a debilitating disease, made the understandable, personal, *and totally legal* choice to keep the fact of his illness to himself and his family.

"Point number three—" Joe held his hand up so everyone in the courtroom could see the three fingers. "His employers discovered his illness. And ladies and gentlemen, the illness I am referring to is AIDS."

Everyone there knew what the case was about, but still a murmur breezed through the courtroom, and the judge frowned. Matt reached over for Miguel's hand and then let it go, and Bud held Sarah's hand tight.

Joe held four fingers high, and when he spoke again he was even quieter, more low-key. "And point number four, they panicked." Mr. Wheeler shook his head, no. "And in their panic they did what most of us would like to do with AIDS: get it and the people who have it as far away as possible."

Miguel muttered something in Spanish that was not polite. Even though Andrew had worked with Joe for weeks on his opening remarks, Andrew still was a little uncomfortable with the way it sounded in the courtroom. Nevertheless, he thought, it was necessary to get the jury to confront their prejudices early in the case.

Joe paused to let the jury consider what he had said. "The behavior of Andrew Beckett's employers may seem reasonable to you." Several of the jurors nodded. "It does to me. After all, AIDS is a deadly, incurable disease—"

"It is not," Miguel whispered to Andrew's mother.

"But," Joe continued, "however you come to judge the behavior of Charles Wheeler and his partners in moral, ethical, or human terms, when they fired Andrew Beckett, *they broke the law*." Joe again paused to let the jury consider what he had said.

This statement seemed to cause some consternation among the defendants, and Mr. Wheeler whispered something to Ms. Conine, who motioned for him to be quiet. Mr. Seidman alone looked thoughtful.

After allowing a few seconds for everyone to consider what he had said, Joe finished by paraphrasing something Judge Garnett mentioned during the failed settlement conference. "And when lawyers break the law, when this society loses respect for the law, our cherished institutions will be burned to the ground, and our children and grandchildren will live like savages." Joe grinned at the judge, who frowned, and then Joe looked at Andrew, who had caught the quote and smiled. "Thank you, Your Honor," Joe said, and he sat down.

"How'd I do?" he whispered to Andrew, and Andrew nodded with approval and then looked off at the marble panels in the wall.

"Ms. Conine," Judge Garnett said, "you may approach the jury, if you wish, to deliver your opening remarks."

Mr. Wheeler whispered something to her, and then Ms. Conine stood. She looked like anyone's pretty, thin, middle-aged mother, or perhaps a favorite sister, her curly black hair falling a bit over her forehead. Her whole appearance and demeanor said: I'm one of you, a mother, a working woman—you can believe me. She had won many cases because juries believed her.

Ms. Conine did not waste time with preliminaries, and she was not interested in even such simple attention-getters as holding up fingers. When she spoke her voice was quiet, calm, controlled, as if it was so obvious that she was on the side of the "truth" that she did not even have to emphasize it. "Fact," she said. "Andrew Beckett's performance on the job ranged from competent—good—to oftentimes me-diocre, sometimes flagrantly incompetent."

Joe gave Andrew a stern look that said, stay seated and shut up, and Andrew grabbed a legal pad and a pen and began writing. Miguel said something in Spanish to Matt, and Matt nodded in agreement, although he did not understand a word of the language. Andrew's parents had never heard their son described in this way and they were shocked; it could not be true, it could not be the Andy they knew, who had always excelled at everything, from school to sailing to tennis.

Ms. Conine gave the jurors a few moments to think and then continued, just as calmly as before. "Fact: He made a critical error on a multi-million-dollar lawsuit.

"Fact: He claims he is the victim of lies and deceit, yet Andrew Beckett *lied* to his employers, going to great efforts to conceal his disease from them with utter disregard for the health and well-being of his co-workers."

Several of the jurors switched their gaze from Ms. Conine to Andrew. Ms. Conine knew she had the jury's attention, and she took full advantage of it, lowering her voice even more so the jurors had to concentrate to hear her.

"Fact: Andrew Beckett was successful in his duplicity. The partners at Wyant, Wheeler did not know he had AIDS when they fired him.

"Fact: AIDS is a heartbreaking tragedy.

"Fact: Andrew Beckett is dying."

Andrew's father held his mother's hand very tightly; this was only the first hour of the first day and already it was difficult to bear.

"Fact: Andrew Beckett is angry. Because his lifestyle — his reckless behavior — has cut short his life. And in his anger, his rage, he's lashing out. He wants someone to pay; specifically, he wants Wyant, Wheeler to pay. But they are not responsible for his illness. Andrew Beckett was fired for his incompetence. Period.

"Thank you."

Ms. Conine went to her chair, and a wave of conversation swept the courtroom. "Oh, I'd like to get her," Miguel said, "and those fat partners," and Matt agreed.

"This is going to be rough," Andrew's father whispered to Sarah. "I hope Andy can take it."

I hope this isn't going to be too hard on Miguel and my family, Andrew thought.

Tough broad, Joe thought.

The first day was not a good day for the plaintiff's case. Joe started by trying to prove that Andrew was an excellent lawyer, and he called witness after witness for whom Andrew had provided excellent representation, usually winning the cases involved, or at least settling them very favorably, but the witnesses were less than enthusiastic although Andrew had performed very well for them. The last witness of the day, Arnold Laird, was typical. He was the general counsel of a large insurance company that Andrew had represented in a multi-million-dollar lawsuit involving alleged fraud on the part of several of the company's officers and directors. Mr. Laird was a large, comfortable man, and he did not like being on the witness stand; he could not look directly at Andrew.

Joe spoke to him from behind the plaintiff's counsel's table — this was not a television courtroom, the attorneys generally remained seated instead of standing menacingly in front of the witness stand. "Andrew Beckett represented your company in a lawsuit in 1990, is that correct?" Joe asked.

"That is correct," Mr. Laird said.

"Were you pleased with his work?"

"We were satisfied with the outcome of the litigation," Mr. Laird said.

Joe and Andrew looked at each other and Andrew made a note on a legal pad; it was becoming very obvious that Wyant, Wheeler's clients did not want to alienate the firm. Joe shook his head and referred to some documents on his table. "Mr. Laird, when I approached you about being a witness at this trial, you gave sworn testimony in a deposition. Is that correct?"

"That is correct," Mr. Laird said properly.

"In that deposition you said you were quote 'impressed and delighted' with Andrew Beckett's work. Do you recall saying that?"

Mr. Laird looked at the defense table, and Charles Wheeler, not at Joe. "In all honesty," he said, "I was delighted with certain aspects of Andy's work, but *in general* I found the work satisfactory."

Joe stared hard at the witness. Why was this happening again? This was the fifth witness who had somehow changed his opinion from a month or so ago. "Mr. Laird," Joe said. "Do you agree that a bologna sandwich is a satisfactory meal, whereas caviar and champagne and roast duck with baked Alaska for dessert might be considered delightful?"

"We object," Jerome Green said from the defense table. The defense's strategy was to preserve Ms. Conine for the important points and, to preserve her credibility with the jury, let other attorneys take care of routine objections and procedural matters. Even so, the attorney picked to handle the "routine" details, Mr. Green, was a senior partner in Wyant, Wheeler's defense firm, Peterson, Lehigh, Monroe, and Smith—something that Ms. Conine dearly wanted to be. And not only was Mr. Green a senior partner, but he was also black, a fact that the defense team hoped would give them even more credibility against Joe.

Mr. Green thought for a moment, then continued. "These gastronomical comments are irrelevant to these proceedings, Your Honor."

"Your Honor," Joe said before the judge had a chance to rule on the objection, "a little while ago this witness characterized Andrew Beckett as caviar and now he's calling him a bologna sandwich. I think the jury has the right to know what powerful force"—Joe turned and looked directly at Charles Wheeler—"has caused him to change his mind."

Judge Garnett was exasperated. It looked as though Joe Miller was going to make something of a circus of his courtroom—in any case he certainly was not going to give up easily—and now he was carrying on about food. "He hasn't changed his mind, Mr. Miller," the judge said. "He's simply amplified his answer. Objection sustained."

Joe was not finished yet. This was certainly the last witness of the day, and he had to make some points with the jury. "All right, Mr. Laird. Explain this to me like I'm a four-year-old: Did Andrew Beckett win your case for you?"

"Yes," Mr. Laird said, "we won."

"Well, congratulations. That must have been a very *satisfactory* experience."

"Objection!" Mr. Green said.

"Sustained," the judge said. "Mr. Miller's last remark will be stricken from the record."

Fine, Joe thought, but the jury won't forget it.

"No more questions, Your Honor," Joe said.

"Court is recessed until nine o'clock sharp tomorrow morning," the judge said.

"All rise!" the bailiff called, and the first day was over.

Neither Andrew's family nor Miguel had ever seen a trial before, and they were not happy with the way it seemed to be going, so Andrew decided to take a few minutes and explain to them what they had seen. Joe needed a beer, or something stronger, and he needed it then. Litigating always exhausted him, and that was in a routine case. God, what have I gotten myself into? he thought. But Joe knew that all this was much harder on Andrew than it was for him, so he stayed, and eventually they all left together.

They were totally unprepared for the scene that greeted

them outside. Huge groups of demonstrators screamed at each other, separated by some very grim-looking police officers. Gay activists shouted, "Hey! Hey! Ho! Ho! Homophobia's got to go!" They were countered by "No rights for sodomites," and, from a small group that obviously had problems with rhyming: "Death to faggots." When a preacher saw Andrew he shouted, "God created Adam and Eve, not Adam and Steve!" Even worse were some of the signs being carried: "God will not *allow* science to cure AIDS" and "GAY = Got AIDS Yet?" were just two of them.

Andrew and Joe tried to rescue Andrew's parents, who were obviously shaken, from the crowd when a reporter pushed her way toward them.

"Do you see this as a gay rights issue?" she shouted at Andrew.

Andrew pushed closer and spoke into her microphone. "I'm not political," Andrew said. "I just want what's fair, what's right."

"But you are gay, aren't you?" the reporter persisted.

"I don't see how that's any of your business," Andrew said, "but yes, I am."

They passed through an entire gauntlet of shouting, unrelenting television reporters. They had microphones thrust into their faces and they were asked very personal questions. Miguel simply refused to say anything—he had promised Andrew he would not insult anyone and he was trying hard not to break his promise—but Andrew's parents did answer some questions, as did Joe. Finally they were able to get into the two cars that Joe had waiting. "See you on the news," Joe called out to the angry mob, and they drove away, leaving the two groups of demonstrators still screaming at each other outside the courthouse.

Joe was at his favorite bar within ten minutes—a mostly working-class pub where beer was the beverage of choice and the bartender would throw you out before he'd make a margarita—where he joined his regular after-work drinking buddies, Filko, and Charley, a beefy Philadelphia cop. Charley actually thought he was pretty liberal for being Joe's friend; in fact, most of Charley's friends on the force thought Charley was *too* liberal. They all talked about sports for a while, which was their excuse for meeting anyway; they knew not to ask Joe about a case when he was in trial. They were discussing the Seventy-Sixers when Joe came on the news on the television above the bar.

"Do you believe that homosexuals deserve special treatment?" the reporter asked him.

"Hell no!" Filko shouted at the television.

Joe answered the reporter. "Angela, we're standing in Philadelphia, the City of Brotherly Love, the birthplace of freedom, where our Founding Fathers authored the Declaration of Independence. I don't remember that glorious document saying all *straight* men are created equal. I could have sworn it says, 'All men are created equal.'"

The reporter started to ask another question, but Joe said, "Thank you, Angela," and walked off camera.

"Give me a goddamned break, Joe!" the cop yelled.

The reporter concluded her story. "This case is sending a cold chill through the legal community here. One of Wyant, Wheeler's key clients, the Grace Foster Foundation, which supports several AIDS charities, has taken its business to another firm until this matter is resolved . . . "

"Hey, Joe," Filko said, "you're not starting to get a little light in the loafers here on us, are you?"

Joe had had enough; he was angry, very angry. "Yes, Filko, I am! I'm on the prowl, Filko. I need a man, a man just like you! How about it, Filko? Want to take a turn on the bottom for a change?"

Filko was startled; he had no response.

"These people make me sick, Filko!" Joe shouted. "But a law's been broken, okay? The *law*. You do remember it, don't you?"

The bartender thought that things were getting too ugly, and he broke in before Filko could respond. "At least we agree on one thing, Joe," he said. "Those frootie tooties make me sick too." He reached up and changed the channel to something less controversial.

Unfortunately, there was more about the case on the other station. Their reporter had caught Andrew's parents. "Excuse me, Mrs. Beckett," the reporter called. "Could we have a word with you, please!"

Sarah turned to face the camera. "How do you think the trial is going?" the reporter asked.

"It's much too early to tell," Sarah said, "but we have every confidence in the outcome."

"How is Andrew holding up under the strain?" the reporter asked.

Andrew's father answered. "Andy's a strong person, and we're a strong family. He's doing fine."

The reporter wanted Sarah, not Bud, on the camera. She thought that talking with a dying man's mother made a better story. "Now that the public knows that your son is gay and that he has AIDS, how does that make you feel?" she asked Sarah.

From his bar stool, Joe smiled to see Miguel on-screen in the background, muttering.

"Listen," Sarah said gently to the reporter. "This is a world filled with wars, famine, poverty, homelessness. And people make a fuss because two men, or two women, want to live together, or make love. It all seems kind of silly, doesn't it?"

Everyone in the bar, except Joe, erupted with boos and catcalls. Joe was quiet, thinking. How many years earlier would these same people, or people like them, have reacted the same way to the thought of equal rights for blacks?

"Hey, Joe!" Filko said. "You're changing on me, and I think it's a goddamned shame."

Joe put down his glass, still half full, and left without another word.

S ix

For as long as Andrew could remember, he had wanted to be a lawyer. His determination did not waver all through undergraduate school, where he majored in political science, considered the appropriate major for anyone planning to go on to law school. His grades were good, his Law School Admission Test scores high, and four years later he was accepted at all of the law schools he applied to. He thrived in law school, making law review on the basis of his grades alone. If one's grades were not high enough to guarantee a position on the review automatically, it was possible to enter a "writing competition," and even though it was not necessary, Andrew entered that too and would have been selected without his high grades. He worked diligently through law school, and, three years later, when he was offered positions in six different firms, chose Wyant, Wheeler, mostly because of Charles Wheeler's reputation as a supreme corporate litigator.

Andrew often laughed about his first day at the firm. The most important thing seemed to be that he learn their billing procedures immediately. Andrew was to bill in tenth-of-an-hour segments, and it was emphasized that it almost always was possible to bill his time to someone. Then, at the end of the day when he was tired, he was taken to have his photograph taken for a book that was distributed to the partners. The book contained a page for each associate, with a brief biography, a list of awards and achievements, and a photograph. It was not until much later that Andrew learned that associates, and some partners, called the book the "Pig Book."

Andrew had never imagined that he would be on the other side of a lawsuit from Wyant, Wheeler, and he had never imagined how tiring it was to be a principal in a case instead of a representative for someone else. As the trial plowed on, Andrew began to look much worse than he had in his photograph in the Pig Book; he lost more weight, the chemotherapy was making more hair fall out, and he was always exhausted. The trial was even wearing on the participants who were healthy: Joe Miller and Belinda Conine were very tired; Charles Wheeler, who looked ten years older than he had when the trial started, was spending his days in court and then going to the office every evening to work on cases for his own clients; Judge Garnett wished he had taken this time to go on his annual vacation to the South Pacific.

Joe finally finished with the stream of witnesses he'd hoped would convince the jury that Andrew was a superb lawyer, and he immediately began on the next part of his case: proving that Walter Kenton knew what KS looked like and that therefore he could have known that Andrew had KS, and therefore AIDS. His main witness in this part of the case was Melissa Benedict, a paralegal from the Washington firm where Mr. Kenton had been a member before he was enticed away by Wyant, Wheeler. It was a fortunate coincidence that Andrew even knew about her. Wyant, Wheeler was local counsel in a case that Mr. Kenton's former firm was litigating in Philadelphia, and Ms. Benedict was brought along to help, although only out of the courtroom, of course, because of her lesions.

After Ms. Benedict had been sworn in, Joe looked at her for a moment, wondering if she too would have a change of memory, as so many of the previous witnesses had. Finally, he began:

"Ms. Benedict, is it correct that you worked for Walsh, Almer, and Brahm three years ago, at the same time as Walter Kenton?"

"That is correct," Ms. Benedict said. She had been a litigation paralegal for almost ten years, so a few minutes on the witness stand did not frighten her.

"And Walter Kenton knew the Kaposi's sarcoma lesions on your face were caused by AIDS?"

The jury studied Ms. Benedict carefully; she looked healthy enough to them.

"Definitely," Ms. Benedict said. "I told all the partners."

Now Joe spoke very slowly and carefully. "How did Walter Kenton treat you after you told him you had AIDS?"

"Every time he came into contact with me, he'd get this look on his face. I called it the 'Oh God' look, as in 'Oh God, here comes that woman with AIDS.'"

Andrew laughed, and Mr. Kenton looked very uncomfortable. Charles Wheeler whispered something to Ms. Conine. Once again, Mr. Seidman seemed to be thinking about the substance of the testimony.

Good, Joe thought. "Thank you," he said to Ms. Benedict. "No more questions, Your Honor."

There was a whispered conference at the defense table, and it was decided that this witness was not important enough to require Ms. Conine's cross-examination so Jerome Green took over.

"Ms. Benedict, how did you contract the AIDS virus?" he asked.

"During a transfusion. I lost a lot of blood giving birth to my second child."

Andrew knew where the questioning was going, and he did not like it; Miguel, in the audience, wondered why the defense counsel asked the question.

"In other words," Mr. Green said, "in *your* case there was no *behavior* on your part that caused you to be infected. It was something you were unable to avoid, isn't that correct?"

Miguel understood now the reason for the question, and he started whispering nasty things about Mr. Green to Andrew's father, who agreed.

"I guess—" Ms. Benedict started.

"Thank you," Mr. Green said.

Ms. Benedict was not about to be intimidated. "But," she said, "I do not consider myself any different from everyone else who has this disease: I'm not guilty, I'm not innocent, I'm just trying to survive." She looked at Andrew, who smiled and gave her a thumbs-up.

From this witness, who had established that Mr. Kenton knew what KS looked like, Joe went to Anthea Burton, a black paralegal at Wyant, Wheeler who had worked closely with Andrew. Her testimony could help establish that Andrew looked as if he had AIDS. In this case, Joe was hoping that two plus two would equal four in the minds of the jurors: Walter Kenton knew what AIDS looked like; Andrew's appearance looked as though he had AIDS; therefore Kenton knew, or at least could have known, that Andrew had AIDS.

Joe handled the preliminary questions carefully, knowing that Ms. Burton was testifying in front of the four senior partners of her firm. He led her gently through questions about how often she was in contact with Andrew, her day-to-day schedule, how often she had contact with the partners, and then got her to confirm that she had seen lesions on his face, although she called them "marks."

"Now tell me, Ms. Burton," Joe continued, "beyond noticing the marks on his face, were there other things about Andrew's appearance that made you suspect he has AIDS?"

"Well, he was getting thinner, and he looked kind of tired sometimes. I knew he was working very hard, but I still thought something was wrong, and I find it difficult to believe that the partners didn't notice anything—"

"Objection!" Ms. Conine broke in.

"Just answer the questions," the judge told Ms. Burton.

Joe was satisfied that the jury had heard what he wanted them to hear and he went on. "Have you ever felt discriminated against at Wyant, Wheeler?"

"Well, yes," Ms. Burton told him after thinking about it for a moment.

"In what way?"

"Well, Mr. Wheeler's secretary, Lydia, told me that Mr. Wheeler had a problem with my earrings."

"Really?" Joe said in mock surprise. Ms. Burton was wearing large, long, dangling earrings.

"Yes," Ms. Burton said. "Apparently, Mr. Wheeler felt that they were too 'ethnic.' That's the word she used. She said Mr. Wheeler would like me to wear something smaller, less garish, 'more American.'"

"What did you say?"

"I said, my earrings *are* American — African-American."

Mr. Wheeler shook his head, no, as if he was denying that it had ever happened.

"Thank you," Joe said. "No more questions, Your Honor."

Ms. Conine took the cross-examination herself. She could not allow Mr. Wheeler to be portrayed as a bigot in front of the jury.

"Ms. Burton," she said quietly. "Were you recently promoted?"

"Yes, I'm now in charge of the entire paralegal department."

"Congratulations on your unfettered ascendance at Wyant, Wheeler," Ms. Conine said.

"But I don't think —"

Ms. Conine interrupted her. "I don't understand, Ms. Burton. How do you explain the promotion of an obviously intelligent, articulate, qualified African-American woman in a firm where discrimination is practiced wantonly and constantly, as Mr. Beckett claims."

"Objection!" Joe yelled.

"I don't know, I guess it's because —" Ms. Burton said at the same time.

"One at a time!" the court stenographer called out, typing furiously.

"Order!" Judge Garnett said. "Overruled," he told Joe. "It's a fair question."

"So how do you explain it?" Ms. Conine asked.

"I can't explain it," Ms. Burton admitted.

Ms. Conine went in for the kill. "Well, could the explanation be that Mr. Wheeler and his partners are not bigots?"

"Objection!" Joe yelled. "Your Honor, Counselor is trying to put words in the witness's mouth."

"Calm down, Mr. Miller," Judge Garnett told him.

"I'll rephrase," Ms. Conine said. "Could it be that these so-called instances of discrimination that Counselor has been trying to establish might just be small misunderstandings that were blown out of all proportion?"

"I think you tend to oversimplify the issues somewhat," Ms. Burton replied, and Andrew thought, Good for her.

"I'll take that under consideration," Ms. Conine said.

"May I be excused now?" Ms. Burton asked the judge.

"Do you have any more questions, Ms. Conine?" he asked.

"No, Your Honor."

"You may step down," the judge told Ms. Burton.

It was the end of a long day at the end of a long week.

———

Fall had come upon Philadelphia, not a cold, wet, dismal fall, as many of them are, but a bold, clear, clean, fragrant fall. Young men played football in the parks; sweaters were seen again; a new class of freshmen was settling into Philadelphia's many institutions of higher learning; and Andrew Beckett was dying. He had a while left, he knew, but he also knew he would never see another fall, probably not even another spring. He found the trial exhausting, and so far all he had done was sit there hour after hour, day after day, and make notes that Joe mostly ignored. The hardest part—his own time on the stand—was yet to come.

Andrew had planned to spend the weekend with Joe preparing for the following week, but when Joe saw how haggard Andrew looked on Friday afternoon he took Andrew's mother aside and suggested that she take Miguel and Andrew home for the weekend. "Don't let him even think about the case," Joe told her. "It's going fine," he said, although he was not sure it was, not sure at all; Joe usually got "signals" from the jury that gave him an idea of how he was doing and the signals he was getting in this case were not good. It was not that the jurors did not believe the case he was presenting, he thought, it was that they didn't care whether it was true or not.

Andrew did go to his parents' home for the weekend, after much cajoling by both of them and Miguel, and it turned out to be one of the most enjoyable times Andrew and Miguel had had together since Andrew had become ill. On Saturday afternoon they went to the beach, and Andrew told Miguel the story about trying to capture a sandpiper for years and then finding one with a broken wing and caring for it until it got well enough to fly away. "That's what I'm going to do for you," Miguel said, "but if you then fly away I'll never forgive you."

Andrew laughed. "You're stuck with me for life, Miguel," he said, and then they were silent, both of them thinking that "life" in this case was short. They walked along the shore, scuffing at pebbles and shells, enjoying the warmth of the fall sun, and then Andrew said, "Let's have a party!"

"A party? Why?" Miguel asked. Parties were the last thing on his mind.

"It would be fun! We haven't had a real party for a long time."

"What kind of party?" Miguel asked. If Andrew wanted a party, they would have a party. He was already considering menus.

"A costume party," Andrew said. "Halloween is coming, and you and I have never been to a costume party together. Let's have one ourselves."

"Oh no," Miguel said. "Drag queens."

"Well maybe one or two," Andrew admitted.

"We'll have to ask Joe," Miguel said, "and his wife."

Andrew tried to imagine Joe meeting a man in drag and he laughed at the idea. "Sure," he said. "Joe's been working awfully hard. He could use a break."

"You know," Miguel said, "I don't really like that guy. He's working hard for you, I know that, but I don't like the way he looks at you."

"It's hard to meet your prejudices face-to-face," Andrew said.

That same beautiful Saturday afternoon Joe spent three hours in his office working on Andrew's case. He reviewed transcripts of some of the trial testimony, reviewed transcripts of depositions of witnesses he expected to be called the following week, read the jurors' questionnaires yet another time, and began to draft answers to questions he thought Andrew was likely to be asked when he was on the stand. Filko was there too, working on an immigration case that he had accepted, reluctantly, the same day that Andrew had first come there. He was mumbling to himself when Joe decided that he was too tired to work anymore, and as Joe passed Filko's desk on his way out, Filko said, "I don't know how I got talked into taking a damned immigration case. I don't know anything about immigration law, and I can't understand my client!"

"Everyone deserves representation," Joe said on his way out the door.

"At least I'm not dumb enough to take on Charles fucking Wheeler," Filko said, but Joe did not hear him.

The thing that had most surprised Joe about his new baby was how many diapers she used. "Doesn't she do anything else?!" he had said earlier in the week, after it was his turn to get up at 4:00 A.M. and change her. Now as he passed a drugstore on the way home he remembered that his wife had asked him to pick up more disposable diapers. I should buy stock in the company, he thought, as he walked into the store.

Joe decided he wasn't going to fool around; he picked up the biggest box of diapers the store had and was looking around for some candy—Joe's love of sweets was his only major vice, if it could be called that—when he saw a young man glance at him, then look away, then look back as if he knew him. The young man was wearing grass-stained sweat clothes and carrying a football, and Joe was sure they had never met.

"How's the trial going?" the young man said.

"Excuse me?" Joe said.

"It's a great case!"

Joe looked puzzled. He still was not sure the young man was talking about Andrew's case.

"I saw you on television," the young man explained. "My name's Mark," he added, "I'm a law student at Penn."

"Oh, so you saw me on television," Joe said. "How're you doing, Mark?" He shook the young man's hand. "Penn's a great school," he said. "Lots of good lawyers have come out of there. What year are you in?"

"Second," Mark said. He seemed to want to talk, but Joe was eager to get home, and he began to move away. "Listen," Mark said, "I just wanted you to know, it's a tremendously important case and you're doing a great job."

"Thanks," Joe told him. "Look, when you get out of school, give me a call. Maybe I can do something for you." He handed the young man a business card, and the young man examined it; he seemed to want to say more.

"Well, Mark, take care," Joe said.

"Listen," Mark said, "would you like to have a drink with me? I just finished a game, and I could use a beer."

Joe was surprised, but he still did not know what was coming. "I really can't," he said. "My wife's expect—"

"I don't pick up people in drugstores every day," the young man interrupted, "but in your case I would make an exception." He laughed and looked a little uncomfortable. As far as he was concerned, Joe was a celebrity and asking him for a date was not easy.

Joe waited until a woman near them moved away before answering. "Do you think I'm"—he lowered his voice to a whisper.—"Gay?"

"Aren't you?" Mark said.

Joe had always had a quick temper, but probably never quicker than at this moment. "What's the matter with you! Do I look gay to you? Jesus!" Joe started to walk away.

"Hey, relax," Mark said. "Do I look gay to you?" It was a fair question. Mark looked like anyone's idea of an all-American young man, complete with the football under his arm.

Joe stopped. "Relax? I ought to kick your faggoty little ass for you!"

"Hey, man, take it as a compliment," Mark said. He still wasn't taking this too seriously.

"Compliment!" Joe yelled. He grabbed the young man's jacket and shook him. "Don't you know this is exactly the kind of bullshit that makes people hate you guys?" He pushed the young man away and hurried down the aisle.

Mark could not believe that Joe had actually grabbed him. It had never happened to him before and the first person to put their hands on him in anger because he was gay was an attorney on the gay side of a very public case. "Asshole!" Mark called. "You want to *try* to kick my ass, Joe? You asshole!"

"You're the asshole, buddy!" Joe yelled back.

"Get a life!" Mark yelled.

Joe was furious, and he was even more furious that people were watching him, and even more furious that people might think he was one of *them*, and he ran through the shoplifting detector without paying for the diapers, setting off a loud buzzer. "Shit!" he said.

A wary security guard said, "Excuse me, Sir, do you wish to purchase that item?" and Mark, watching, laughed, shrugged, and walked away.

Hours later, Joe was still angry. Lisa was trying to work on a new painting, and she was tired of hearing Joe's ranting. They had worked hard for their educations and their decent middle-class life, and now Joe was carrying on about gay people like some redneck, and Joe, she thought, of all people, should understand discrimination. When they had first moved into their mainly white suburb, they were not welcome, but over the last six years their neighbors had gradually come to accept them. It had not been easy at first, however, and Lisa did not like to hear Joe talking about another group the same way she was sure that they had been talked about — and perhaps still were — by some of the more conservative people in their neighborhood. Still, Joe would not leave the topic alone. "But what was it?" he said again. "What was this guy thinking?"

"I don't know, Joe," Lisa told him, for at least the tenth time.

"Is there some kind of expression I've picked up from Beckett? Some kind of attitude I've unconsciously adopted? Am I walking different? Am —"

"How does Beckett walk different, Joe?" Lisa asked.

"I don't know," Joe answered impatiently. "Have I picked up some kind of vocal thing? Some kind of homo vibes?"

This was so unlike the Joe that Lisa thought she knew, and she didn't like it very much. "You know," she said, "women get hit on like that three hundred and sixty-five days a year. It happens to you *once* and it's earth shattering? Get over it."

"But, but . . . " Joe recognized the expression in his wife's voice for what it was: trouble. "I had a box of Pampers under my arm, for Christsake."

Lisa concentrated on her painting and did not answer.

"You know, Beckett's 'lover,' as he calls him, is an artist too," Joe said.

"What else should he call him?" Lisa asked.

"I don't know. 'Lover' just seems like he's trying to throw it in people's faces."

This was getting to be too much. "Get over it, Joe," Lisa said again. "Come on, let's go to bed. I'm tired, and you're going to be in that office of yours again all day tomorrow."

They shut out the lights downstairs and went upstairs and checked on the baby, who was sleeping beautifully, and they got ready for bed and turned out the lights. Joe was asleep within minutes. But Lisa was wide awake, wondering why Joe was so blind about this one topic. She shook him a little, and he mumbled something but did not wake up.

She shook him again. "Joe? Honey?"

"Okay, okay, I'll change her," he said.

"Wake up," Lisa said. "It's not that."

"Huh?" Joe said, his voice heavy with sleep.

"Now tell me again," Lisa said. "What is it you find so disgusting about two men making love?" She started unbuttoning Joe's pajama top.

God, Joe thought, would she ever give up? But the unbuttoning might lead to something. "A guy putting his dick in another guy's mouth. It's just disgusting."

Lisa kissed Joe's chest, nuzzling a little. "Okay, so help me with this one. Is it disgusting to put your penis into someone's mouth? Or is it disgusting to take someone's penis in your mouth?" She worked her way down to his stomach, then said, "I'm just curious," then went a little lower.

This definitely had possibilities, Joe thought. "Which answer will get me what I want?" he said.

Lisa stopped short, pulled herself up and put her head on her pillow.

"Was that the wrong answer?" Joe asked.

"Yeup. Good night."

———

Monday morning Joe began to deal with the missing complaint and how it might have become missing. His first witness was Shelby, Andrew's former secretary, and as soon as she saw Andrew watching her testify and saw how bad he looked she started crying, even as she continued to speak.

"We were going crazy looking for that complaint. I thought I was in the Twilight Zone."

She paused for a moment, trying to compose herself, then continued: "Mr. Beckett was actually screaming at everybody, and he was always so nice. And then he looked so freaky, and then Mr. Kenton showed up suddenly although no one had called him and he kept saying to Mr. Beckett, 'You *lost* the Highline complaint.' Then Mr. Beckett yelled at him and he called Mr. Wheeler, and then

Jamey came running up to me with it in his hand and said it was packed up to be shipped to Central Files."

"Central Files?" Joe asked.

"That's the place paperwork is sent when cases are closed. Then Jamey ran it over to court and everybody just stood there completely wasted. And Mr. Beckett kept saying, 'I'm sorry, I'm sorry. I just don't understand it.'" Shelby did not understand it either. There were several steps of paperwork to be completed before a case file could be closed and sent for storage, not the least of which was that a final bill had to be completed. Shelby broke down completely then, and Andrew wanted to get up and put his arm around her and tell her it was okay, all she had to do was tell the truth, and she had. Joe pulled a handkerchief from his pocket and said, "Your Honor, may I?"

"Certainly," Judge Garnett said. Just as Ms. Conine went home every evening and told her husband how much she hated the case, the judge also went home every evening and told his wife how much he hated the case. He did not understand why Andrew was putting himself through this, when he did not have much of a case, and he felt sorry for Andrew's family sitting there day after day and hearing witnesses saying less than complimentary things about their son and brother—the judge did not allow himself to think "and lover." And now witnesses were sobbing on the stand.

Joe got up and walked to the witness stand and handed Shelby his handkerchief.

"Thank you," Shelby said. She wiped her eyes and blew her nose and after a minute or two was more or less composed again.

Joe stayed where he was, knowing he was breaking the rules. "Are you okay?" he asked.

"Yes," Shelby said.

"Do you want a glass of water?"

"No, thank you."

"Was Andrew Beckett a good boss?" Joe asked.

"Sure!" Shelby said. "He was sweet."

"I mean, as his secretary, how would you characterize Mr. Beckett's work?"

"How should I know? I'm no lawyer, I just worked for him."

Andrew laughed, and then some others in the audience laughed too; even Mr. Wheeler chuckled, and when he did the other senior partners all followed his lead and smiled or laughed a little too.

Mr. Green did not like this sudden warmth between Joe and a witness. "Your Honor, is this for the record?" he asked.

The judge knew what was making Mr. Green uncomfortable. "Mr. Miller, please return to the counsel's table."

Joe returned to his seat and then finished his questioning. "Ms. O'Hara, were you aware that the senior partners had any problem with Mr. Beckett's work prior to the episode of the 'missing' file?"

Shelby was actually startled by the question. "With Mr. Beckett? No, I wasn't!" Andrew's parents smiled at each other.

"Thank you," Joe said. "Your Honor, I have no more questions for this witness."

There was a brief pause while Joe looked at his notes for the next witness, and during that time Joe also studied the jury. The ex-Marine was going to be a real problem, and since he was the first juror picked, he was also the foreman. All through the trial whenever a witness said something positive about Andrew he frowned, and when the defense scored a point he often nodded. Joe knew he was going to have to find a way to sway that one juror if he wanted to win the case. He looked back at his notes again and then asked Andrew a question.

Finally the moment Jamey Collins had been dreading arrived: He was called as a plaintiff's witness. Jamey was noticeably uneasy on the stand, but the questioning started easy, building background about his education, his responsibilities at Wyant, Wheeler, and the frequency of contact with Andrew. Then the questions became tougher.

"Mr. Collins, is Andrew Beckett the kind of lawyer who misplaces crucial documents?"

"Not to my knowledge, no," Jamey said. He looked at Andrew with irritation, as though it were Andrew's fault he was being questioned.

"Mr. Collins," Joe said very deliberately, "if you wanted to make a lawyer look incompetent, would this be a good way to do it? Hiding a document for a few hours, making it look as if the responsible lawyer has misplaced it?"

Jamey did not like the direction this line of questioning was taking, but he thought he could divert it. "Why would Mr. Wheeler and the others behave so outrageously? Because they found out Andy was sick? We have lawyers who've had heart attacks, ulcers. No one has sabotaged them—" Jamey's forehead was shiny with perspiration and Joe wondered why he was so nervous.

"Did you have something to do with this file being lost accidentally—on purpose?" Joe asked while Jamey was still answering the last question.

"Objection!" Ms. Conine yelled.

"I'll rephrase," Joe said. "Did you have anything to do with this file being"—Joe stopped and seemed to be considering the right word—"misplaced?"

"Absolutely not," Jamey said.

That was a possibility that Andrew had not considered, and he looked at Jamey intently. So did Joe. He stared in silence for an uncomfortably long time, and Jamey squirmed in his seat. Finally Joe stood, without permission from the judge, and asked his final question:

"Are you a homosexual?"

Jamey wanted time to think. "What?" he said.

"C'mon, Mr. Collins, are you a homosexual? You know, gay?"

The courtroom erupted. The activists in the audience

booed and hissed; the Wyant, Wheeler team shouted their outrage; the jurors whispered among themselves and looked confused; Mr. Wheeler looked as though he had been personally insulted. Andrew thought, This is it, he's alienated everyone and I've lost the case; what *is* Joe doing?

Judge Garnett was not pleased. "Hold it!" he yelled. "Hold it!"

"Objection!" Ms. Conine yelled. "Where has this come from? Suddenly counsel is attacking his own witness. Mr. Collins's sexual orientation has absolutely no relevance to this case!"

The Wyant, Wheeler team all nodded their approval, and there were more outbursts from the spectators.

"I said HOLD IT!" Judge Garnett yelled, and gradually the courtroom quieted. "Now, Mr. Miller," the judge said when the courtroom was finally completely quiet, "could you kindly share with me exactly what's going on in your brain" — your tiny, pea-size brain, the judge thought — "because I don't have a clue at the moment."

Neither do I, Andrew thought.

Joe turned to look at Andrew, and then turned back to the judge. "Your Honor, everyone in this courtroom is thinking about sexual preference, sexual orientation, whatever you want to call it. They're thinking about who does what with whom and how they do it. They're certainly looking at Mr. Beckett and thinking about it. They're probably looking at Mr. Wheeler, Ms. Conine, and even you, Your Honor, and wondering about it."

Ms. Conine turned a little pink, the first time she had been flustered at all during the trial, and she turned to the side and studied the pattern in the marble under the windows. The Wyant, Wheeler partners all looked sympathetically at Mr. Wheeler.

"What's going on?" Andrew's father whispered to Andrew's mother, and Sarah whispered back, "I don't know."

Jesus, Andrew thought, he *wants* to lose this case, and on that point Ms. Conine would have agreed.

"I know they're looking at me and wondering about it, Your Honor," Joe said. "So let's get it out in the open— out of the closet—because we're not just talking about AIDS here. Let's be honest about what this case is really about: the general public's hatred, our loathing, our *fear* of homosexuals, and how that climate of hate translated into the firing of this particular homosexual, my client, Mr. Beckett." Andrew noted that Joe used "our," which included Joe himself, instead of "its," which could have excluded him, but he thought that it was probably more effective for the jurors to have them think that Joe was one of them.

"Would you please take a seat, Mr. Miller," the judge said.

Joe sat behind his table, and the courtroom was totally silent while the judge considered his answer. "Good," Andrew mouthed to Joe. Ms. Conine and Mr. Wheeler sat without moving. Miguel stared hard at Jamey.

Finally the judge spoke: "Mr. Miller, in this courtroom justice is blind to matters of race, creed, color, and sexual orientation."

Joe was not ready to give up. He wanted his question answered. "With all due respect, Your Honor, we don't live in this courtroom, do we?"

"No, Mr. Miller, we don't," the judge answered. "However, as regards this witness, I'm going to sustain the defense's objection."

"In that case, Your Honor, I have no further questions," Joe said, and Jamey Collins had never felt quite so relieved about anything in his life.

"Very good," Andrew told Joe.

The plaintiff's next witness was important: Walter Kenton. Joe needed to establish not only that Kenton could have known that Andrew had AIDS because Mr. Kenton knew Ms. Benedict from his former firm in Washington, but also he needed to establish, if he could, that Kenton was homophobic. He certainly did look like a smug, rich, conservative bastard, Joe thought, and he hoped he could trick Mr. Kenton into exposing that to the jury.

Joe started with the usual questions about Kenton's background and the frequency of his contact with Andrew, and then he asked a totally unexpected question—one that he knew the answer to.

"Tell me, Mr. Kenton, were you ever in the service?"

The lawyers on the Wyant, Wheeler team all looked at each other, surprised by the question and unsure where Joe was heading.

"Yes, Sir, the United States Navy," Mr. Kenton answered proudly.

"And did you ever go to sea?"

"Yes, all the time."

"So tell me," Joe said, "how many weeks at a time would you be out to sea, without stopping at port?"

"Anywhere from two weeks to several months," Mr. Kenton answered.

"Any women on board?" Joe asked.

Mr. Kenton looked at the ex-Marine juror and then back at Joe. "Not when *I* was in the Navy!" he said, and he sounded as though there still would not be any women on naval ships if he had anything to say about it.

Ms. Conine listened intently. Now she thought she knew why Joe was pursuing this line of questioning, and she hoped Mr. Kenton would just answer calmly and rationally.

"So," Joe said, "during those long voyages, months at a time, out to sea, no women in sight, a hundred or more hard-working, robust young men in the prime of their life, at the peak of their natural appetites, their God-given hormonal instincts — anything going on?"

Why is he doing this? Andrew thought.

"Going on? Like what?" Mr. Kenton said. He did not care for the question.

"Like, oh, two sailors playing hide the salami."

"Objection!" Ms. Conine said.

Andrew covered his face with his hands, and in the audience his brother Matt laughed.

"Mr. Miller!" the judge warned sternly, but Mr. Kenton could not resist answering. "We had one guy like that."

"You haven't ruled on my objection, Your Honor," Ms. Conine said.

Judge Garnett considered this. He thought he knew what Joe was doing and he really did not care for it, but he held back since he had previously ruled that Joe could not ask witnesses about their own sexuality. If he consistently ruled out an entire area of testimony, he might be laying grounds for an appeal, and no judge likes to be overruled by a higher court. "Go on, Mr. Miller," he said reluctantly.

"Thank you, Your Honor," Joe said. "Mr. Kenton, when you said you had one guy 'like that' did you mean homosexual?"

"If that's what it's called," Mr. Kenton said with disgust. "He strutted around quarters naked, trying to get everyone to notice him. It made everyone sick, and it was destroying our morale. So we let him know this behavior was unacceptable."

"How did you do that?" Joe asked politely. "Did you write him a letter?" This line of questioning had already yielded much more than Joe had expected. And now Mr.

Kenton made Joe's point better than Joe ever could have made it.

"No," Mr. Kenton answered. "We stuck his head in the latrine—after ten of us had used it."

I cannot believe Joe got a hostile witness to help his case that much, Andrew thought, and he nodded in approval.

"You taught him a lesson?" Joe continued.

Don't answer, Ms. Conine thought.

"Yes, we did," Mr. Kenton said proudly.

"Like firing Andrew Beckett taught *him* a lesson?"

Touché, Andrew thought.

"Objection!" Ms. Conine and Mr. Green called out simultaneously.

"I'll withdraw," Joe said quickly. He had made his point, well. "You were aware," he continued immediately, "that when you worked with Melissa Benedict, she had AIDS, correct?"

"*She* didn't try to conceal it," Mr. Kenton said. He was becoming irritated with this upstart ambulance chaser questioning *his* morals and integrity, and he looked at his partner Charles for encouragement, and Mr. Wheeler smiled and nodded.

"So you *are* aware of the difference between a lesion and a bruise, is that correct?"

Mr. Kenton did not answer the question. "Beckett told me he'd been hit by a racquetball. I believed him."

"Didn't you avoid contact with Ms. Benedict after you found out she had AIDS? She says you acted repulsed by her and you avoided her, is that correct?"

Mr. Kenton answered with as much indignity as he could muster. "I felt, and still feel, nothing but the deepest sympathy and compassion for people like Melissa, who have contracted this terrible disease through no fault of their own."

"It was *not* Drew's fault," Miguel whispered to Sarah, and she whispered back, "I know."

Joe thought about pursuing the questioning, but it was late in the day and he was tired, plus he did not want to hammer the jury too hard on the point of whether it is different if one gets AIDS sexually or otherwise. "No more questions, Your Honor."

"Ms. Conine?" the judge asked.

Ms. Conine wanted time to prepare her witness. "I'd like to reserve until tomorrow, Your Honor."

"In that case," Judge Garnett said, "court is adjourned until nine tomorrow morning."

Almost every night after court Andrew wrote briefs for Joe on various points of law. Joe only referred to the briefs occasionally, because now that they were in trial the day-to-day strategy depended more on the witnesses' testimony than on small legal points. But Joe knew that the writing and thinking kept Andrew from worrying too much about the case, or about his own condition, so Joe encouraged Andrew's research. Occasionally he really did need help and requested research and a memo on a particular legal point he hadn't considered or didn't know much about.

The evening after Mr. Kenton's testimony was one of the times when Joe really did need help with something, and Andrew started work almost as soon as he and Miguel got home from court. It was also the time for Andrew's drip, as they called the IV treatments Andrew received every other day through his catheter. Andrew had finally had a catheter implanted and Miguel had learned how to start and regulate the IV, so now Andrew could take treatments at home in the evenings. Even though it was more convenient, and not as painful, he still hated them, and he was not a very good patient.

"What'd you think of Kenton's testimony?" he asked Miguel. Andrew was sitting in a comfortable leather chair reading a law book while a *Bewitched* rerun played on the television across the room. Andrew had never cared for television and seldom watched it, but Miguel loved reruns of the sitcoms from the sixties and seventies.

"I'd like to see him try to push my head in a toilet!" Miguel said, and then added something in Spanish. He was looking at a large chart on the wall, which helped him keep track of all the various medications Andrew took both orally and intravenously. "Drew, if we start at eight, we'll be done by midnight," he said.

"Yeah, great," Andrew said, but he was not really paying attention.

Miguel got the IV bag from the refrigerator and the equipment he needed from the kitchen counter and hung the bag on the IV pole. He clamped on a needle, unbound the catheter and cleaned it well with alcohol, then inserted the needle while Andrew continued to work on his memo for Joe; he did not look up. After the tubes were connected Miguel stood and examined the bag, but nothing was dripping into the little chamber that regulated the flow. "Drew, it's not going through," he said.

"We may have to flush it again," Andrew said, distracted.

"No, Drew, the vein's closed. We've gotta call Barbara."

"Barbara—Nurse Ratchett? Why?"

"We've got to tell her to come over," Miguel said. "You've got to have your medication!" Miguel was never the calmest of people, and where Andrew and AIDS were concerned he was not calm at all. He went to the phone.

"Look," Andrew said, "I have too much work to do. Let's just skip the treatment for tonight."

"We're not skipping this treatment!" Miguel said. "Dr. Gillman says you have to have it!"

"Look, Miguel, it's my arm and it's my treatment, so let's just skip it!"

Miguel sat facing Andrew. "You want to know something very interesting?" he said. "Fuck you!"

" 'Interesting'?" Andrew said.

"It's interesting to me," Miguel said.

"Yeah, and fuck you too, boyfriend. This stuff obviously is not doing me any good anyway."

Miguel was getting angrier. "This stuff is saving your life, you asshole!"

Andrew looked up with exasperation. This was obviously going to be one of these nights when Miguel was not going to let him get any work done. "What's wrong with you tonight?" he asked.

"Close the law book!" Miguel ordered.

"Just let me finish this—"

"Close the fucking law book!" Miguel shouted, and he grabbed it from Andrew and hurled it across the room.

"Well, the book is closed," Andrew said calmly. Miguel hated it when Andrew would not fight back. "Now what would you like me to do?"

"Drew, the least you can do is look at me while I'm sticking this stuff in your arm. You can forget the fucking case for one hour a day and give me a little of your time."

"Miguel," Andrew said gently, "you think that we don't have much time left, don't you?" Andrew thought so too, but he would never admit it.

"That's not what I said," Miguel told him.

"You're scared. You think that we're running out of time," Andrew said.

"No!" Miguel yelled, and he got up and went to the kitchen and began chopping vegetables furiously.

"You want me to start planning my memorial service?" Andrew said. "You want me to 'begin to prepare for the inevitable'?"

"Maybe you should think about it," Miguel said.

"What's that supposed to mean?"

Oh God, not tonight, Miguel thought. "It means maybe you should think about it."

Andrew went into the kitchen and began to attack another pile of vegetables with a Chinese cleaver.

"No?" Miguel said.

"No! No! No! No! No!" Andrew yelled.

"That's a good answer," Miguel said, coming to the counter where Andrew was still chopping vegetables. "In fact, that's a great answer. We're on the positive plan. You don't have a fatal disease, you have a manageable illness." Miguel did not remember that he had been saying the same thing and believing it only a few months earlier.

"I am not going to give up," Andrew said. "I am not going to let this thing turn us into victims."

"That's the stupidest thing I've ever heard," Miguel said. "What are we, the winners?" Miguel picked up a glass and used it like a microphone. "Ladies and gentlemen, the first prize of AIDS goes to Andrew Beckett and his lover, Miguel." He put down the glass and said, "Excuse me, I'm not your lover, I'm your care partner. Fuck you!" Miguel turned to the stove.

"Look," Andrew said, "I'm sorry. It's just that I'm not ready, it's not my time."

"To what?" Miguel asked.

"I'm not ready," Andrew repeated.

"Say it!" Miguel suddenly yelled.

"To die," Andrew said very quietly.

"Do you think I'm ready for it?" Miguel shouted. "I hate this shit!" He swept bottles, tubes, syringes, bandages off the counter with his arm. "I'm not a fucking martyr! I hate every goddamned part of this! But we've got to *talk* about it!" Miguel could prevent it no longer, and he started to cry, softly at first, then more urgently. "Jesus Christ, it's just not fair. You think I want to lose you? Oh, Drew, I'm so sorry, I'm —"

Andrew reached out and held Miguel gingerly at first, then more tightly. "I'm sorry too," he said.

"I love you so much," Miguel said, trying without succeeding to control his tears.

"I'm just scared," Andrew said. "I am so terribly scared."

Miguel put his arms around Andrew and said, "I love you so much, and you'll always have me."

"I know," Andrew said, trying not to cry himself. "I'm sorry I upset you, Miguel, so sorry."

They held each other for a moment and then suddenly, Andrew heard Joe's voice from the other room.

"Hey, that's Joe!" Andrew said.

"I know," Miguel said, and they rushed back into the living room where Joe was on television.

It was Joe's new commercial. "Are you tired of having doors shut in your face, just because you're disabled? You know you can do the job but they won't give you a chance? There's nothing you can do, right? Wrong! You don't have to settle for closed doors and a cloudy future just because you're physically, emotionally, or mentally challenged, or because of your sex, race or sexual orientation—"

"This is Joe Miller?!" Miguel said, and Andrew put his finger to his lips and went, "Shhh!"

"—I'm attorney Joe Miller of MacReady and Shilts Legal Services, where we are dedicated to stamping out discrimination in this country, one lawsuit at a time. If an employer fires you because of a handicap, if a landlord throws you out because he doesn't like the church you belong to, if you've lost your job for no good reason, you may be entitled to money damages—"

"That's the Joe I know," Andrew interjected. "Shhh!" Miguel said.

"So call me, attorney Joe Miller of MacReady and Shilts. I'll get cash justice for you!"

"I don't believe this," Miguel said. "I think this trial is good for him," he added.

"We'll see how much his attitude has changed when he comes to the party next weekend," Andrew said.

"I'll make sure he has fun," Miguel told him. "I forgot

to tell you, my sister called when you were in the shower. She's coming down from New York for the party, and she's bringing a couple of surprise guests."

"Who?"

"She wouldn't say. She just said they'd be a surprise."

"Not like that crazy artist she brought once, I hope," Andrew said. "You know, the one who said Americans couldn't do anything right."

"No," Miguel said, "he went back to Belgium to cause trouble there."

"Good place for him," Andrew said.

"You know, Drew, there are going to be a lot of people at this party. Everyone's accepted." Miguel put his arm across Andrew's shoulders. "Are you sure you're up to it?" he asked.

"Bring 'em on, I'm ready!" Andrew said.

"You know something, Drew?"

"What?"

"I love you."

As he had so often, Andrew thought, How am I so lucky? "I love you too, Miguel."

They were quiet for a moment, and then Andrew said, "Miguel?"

"Yes."

"Want to try that drip again?"

Seven

"Well, Captain, how do I look?" Andrew asked as he finished buttoning his uniform jacket, his costume for their party.

"You look great, Admiral!" Miguel said.

The two of them wore naval dress whites, and they were very handsome. Andrew had used a little makeup so he didn't look so pale, but he had also rested as much as he could for the last few days, not working on legal points when he got home from the trial, just taking his treatments and listening to music. All that opera was driving Miguel a little nuts, but he said nothing because he liked it when Andrew relaxed. Andrew had not even complained when Miguel said he was going to hire help, not only for the party itself but to clean and prepare beforehand. Andrew had gone to the hospital that day for a blood transfusion because his hemoglobin and platelets were way down.

The first guests arrived all at once: two men dressed as

horrible caricatures of the Ugly American tourist, with cameras and guidebooks and bags; Adam and Eve, with a very real, good-sized boa constrictor; and Miguel's sister, Gabriela, along with her surprise guests — Quentin Crisp, the Flirtations — a gay male vocal quartet, the drag queen Lipsynka, and the singer Q Lazarus.

"You know these people?" Miguel said, astonished. His sister had always been the most conservative of the siblings and was a vice president in the New York office of a Spanish bank.

"Of course," she said, and she introduced everyone to Andrew and then took her guests on a short tour of the loft. Mr. Crisp said it was more space than he'd ever lived in in his life, and Lipsynka looked for the most dramatic way to make her entrance, because she had brought music and intended to perform.

The loft filled rapidly, many guests in costumes so good that Andrew and Miguel could not tell who was under them, and it was not until the party had been going on for a while that Miguel asked Andrew, "Where's Joe?"

Joe and Lisa were not getting a good start. There were all the instructions to the baby-sitter that had to be written down — slightly less complicated than the Book of Numbers in the Old Testament, but only slightly. Then there were the costumes. Lisa was going as a sandwich, a large Swiss cheese and tomato sandwich, but Joe said he was not wearing any faggotty costume. "You've got to do something," Lisa said.

"Yeah, I'm doing something. I'm going."

"Joe!"

"All right," he said, and he got an old brief from his desk and began stapling pages of it all over his suit.

"Joe, what are you doing! You're ruining a perfectly good suit!"

"I'm a lawsuit," Joe said, "now let's go before I change my mind."

"Joe," Lisa said, "why are you carrying a briefcase?"

"Beckett will be on the stand on Monday, and I want to go over some questions with him."

"Joe, at a party?"

"Look, I'm going, aren't I?"

Lisa did not think this was going to be a good night. "All right," she said, "bring your damn papers, but let's go."

They arrived outside Andrew's loft just as some of the earlier guests were leaving. "I knew it," Lisa said, "we're too late."

"Not late enough," Joe muttered, but Lisa ignored him, seeing Adam and Eve pass them in the hall.

"Joe! That snake was alive! This is going to be a great party!"

"Great," Joe echoed weakly.

Andrew was having more fun than he'd had in a long time, certainly more than he'd had since he had been diagnosed, and it was, everyone agreed, a great party—and that was even before the entertainment Gabriela had invited began performing.

"Oh look," Andrew said, "there's Joe. Joe!" Joe and Lisa pushed their way toward him. "I was beginning to think you wouldn't make it," Andrew said.

"Are you kidding? We wouldn't miss it," Lisa said.

"Andy, this is my wife, Lisa."

Andrew shook hands and said, "And this is my lover, Miguel. And this is Miguel's sister, Gabriela. She brought the entertainment."

Everyone exchanged pleasantries, but Joe was thinking about the "entertainment." If Miguel's *sister* arranged it, it probably wasn't some gay thing, but these days who could tell?

"May I get you a drink?" Miguel's sister asked.

"No, I'll take care of him," Andrew said. "Come on, Joe, I'll show you the bar."

"Don't get lost," Joe told Lisa.

"Don't worry," Miguel told him. "I'll take good care of her. Let me show you around," he said to Lisa.

"About that drink," Joe said, and he and Andrew went toward the kitchen. "You seem better, more alive," Joe said.

"I had a blood transfusion today, and I feel great!" Andrew said.

The thought of a blood transfusion was too horrible for

Joe, and he quickly changed the subject. "What do you think about my costume?"

Andrew looked at Joe carefully. He had papers stapled all over himself.

"I'm a lawsuit!" Joe said. "Get it?" Now he was glad he had worn some kind of costume.

"Not bad," Andrew told him.

"But, you get it?"

"Not bad," Andrew said again. "What do you want to drink?"

"Do you have a glass of wine?"

"That's it! A glass of wine! I always had you pegged as a Scotch or bourbon man."

"Well, we've got to go over your Q and A's."

"Fine, but now I'm at a party. We'll get to it later."

Then Joe's worst fears were realized: A man dressed as Mona Lisa came over and said, "Joe Miller!"

Joe took a step back. "Do I know you?"

"Mona Lisa," he said.

"Lawsuit," Joe said, and Mona Lisa drifted off.

"Hey, Joe, relax, have some fun," Andrew told him.

"Why, do you think I'm uncomfortable?"

"Yes, I do," Andrew said.

"You're damned skippy I am," Joe said.

Chandra, Andrew's friend who had taught him how to use makeup, came up to them. "Admiral, you're needed," she said.

"Thanks," Andrew said. "I'll be right there. Joe, you're on your own. Have fun!"

Joe stayed by the bar and did not speak to anyone. What a freak show, he thought. A man dressed as a vaudevillian comedian came up and looked at some of the legal papers stapled to Joe's jacket. "I get it," he said, "you're a lawsuit."

"It was my idea," Joe said.

A woman dressed as a baby came by. "Hi, Joe."

"Iris?" Joe said. Everybody's crazy, he thought, even his secretary.

Joe had never been more uncomfortable in his life, and whenever he tried to join Lisa she was always with an entire group of outrageously dressed guests laughing and carrying on, so he quickly drifted off again.

Joe finally found a corner by a closet door where most of the light came from a group of votive candles burning on a windowsill and as he finally relaxed with his drink—he had changed to Scotch—he heard rustling and laughter from inside the closet. He got up quickly and left the room. The party was everything that Andrew had wanted, and much more, due to Miguel's sister, and when the Flirtations gathered in front of the room and began singing, "Mr. Sandman," Andrew put his arm around Miguel and said, "I've got my dream."

"Me too," Miguel said, and gave Andrew a kiss. The few people who noticed all smiled, happy that Andrew was having such a good time.

Joe finally found Lisa more or less alone just as the Flirtations started singing, and he grabbed her hand and said, "This isn't so bad." He even felt comfortable enough to give Lisa a little kiss. He particularly loved "Mr. Sandman," because he used to listen to it with his first serious high school girlfriend, although he could not tell Lisa that. Then, just as he was deciding that maybe a gay party wasn't so bad after all, he started to listen to the words and realized that they had been changed to make the song very gay. He shook his head and Lisa laughed. The Flirtations finished and Lipsynka came on and started singing "Bad Bad Girl," to the immense delight of the crowd, and Joe thought that she was quite good until he realized something. "That's a man!" Joe said, shocked that he had not known, and Lisa turned toward him, smiled, and nodded. "Christ!" Joe said, and someone near them frowned and said, "Shhh!"

When Lipsynka was finished Andrew climbed the steps to the balcony overlooking the living room, took a small microphone, and called out, "Okay, everybody, it's Madison time!" and the crowd cheered its approval and immediately began forming a long line. Then the music came on, and Andrew called the dance.

"Oh, do you hear that sound, everybody?

"That means it's Madison time!

"Yeah, put yourself in a big, strong line — you're looking good!

"Now when I say 'hit it' I want to see the Big T and the Einstein,

"And then back and do the Madison!

"Ready?"

The crowd looked up at him.

"Hit it!"

Everyone knew the steps and the line executed them with precision. Andrew, for the first time that evening, for the first time in a very long time, completely forgot his disease and was totally immersed in the moment.

"Two points!" he called. *"You're looking fine.*

"Now this time when I say 'hit it' I want to see the Big M, that's the Big M.

"And then I want to see you erase it, and go back to the Madison.

"Are you ready?"

The crowd yelled, "Yes!"

"Hit it!" Andrew called.

The dancers parted, came together, parted again, and came back to a line.

"Well, there's only one word I could use to describe that: Crazy!"

"Crazy!" some of the dancers echoed.

"Come on, Joe, let's dance," Lisa shouted above the noise of the crowd.

"I can't do that," Joe said.

"Just follow me and you'll be fine, and now it's time to join that line," Lisa sang.

"Jesus," Joe said as he was pulled to the end of the line of dancers.

Andrew gave Joe a wave from above, waited for the music to come around again, and addressed his next call directly to Joe and Lisa.

"Now this time when I say 'hit it' I want to see those big Philly hips shaking, that's the Big Philly Hips.

"And then go back to the Philly Ten on the Madison.

"Are you ready?"

"We're ready!" the crowd shouted back.

The music came back to the top.

"Hit it!"

"I can't believe I'm doing this," Joe whispered.

"Smile, dear," Lisa told him.

I can't believe Joe's doing this, Andrew thought, and he swayed to the music and watched the crowd. They were good! And Miguel looked so handsome. For the first time in months he looked really happy.

"Okay, it looked beautiful and it sounded beautiful too.

"I hate to admit it, there's no getting around it.

"All right, now this time when I say 'hit it' I want to see those concealed handguns.

"Yeah, those concealed handguns, please."

The music was not quite back to the top yet.

"And when I say 'hit it' but only when I say 'hit it.'

"So I just guess I'm going to have to say...

"Hit it!"

I can do this, Joe thought, and he watched Lisa and the others carefully, and he copied them perfectly.

Incredible, Andrew thought, what a great party!

"Crazy, people, crazy! And oh so very good!

"And this time is the last time, friends.

"So swing and make it count!

"I want to see the Big M, and I wanna see it erased.

"When I say 'hit it' make it count, make it crazy!

"Hit it!"

Joe had figured out the last move and now they were changing!

"Pretty good!" Lisa said, and then they were back in line.

All the dancers were back in line.

And that was the Madison.

"That's crazy! Crazy!

"And hold it right there and give yourselves a big hand!"

Andrew waved the microphone and the guests, dancers and observers, whistled and applauded. "Hey Andy! Yeah Andy!" they yelled, and Andrew waved again and started down the stairs.

Miguel could not keep tears from his eyes, and Chandra saw and squeezed his hand. "He was great, wasn't he?"

"I'm going to miss him so much," Miguel said.

After that, Joe was more comfortable and Andrew introduced him to several of his gay friends, one of them in drag. Joe, of course, had trouble with pronouns — He? She? *It?* — and then the lights were dimmed and the last entertainer, Q Lazarus, sang "Heaven," beautifully and quietly. At first everyone just listened, but then Miguel took Andrew in his arms and started dancing and gradually everyone joined. All eyes were on Miguel and Andrew, dancing slowly, gracefully, so obviously in love, and by the end of the song few of those eyes were dry.

The party broke up soon after the slow dance. It was still early, but the mood had become too intimate: People felt as though they had witnessed a personal scene they were not meant to see. Andrew was elated, and everyone sensed his good mood. "Some of the others are going to a club. Want to go?" Miguel asked, and Andrew gave him a kiss and said, "No, you go. I promised Joe I'd look at some things."

"Then I'll stay too," Miguel said.

"Miguel, look at me." Andrew took Miguel's hands. "Go," he said quietly.

Miguel thought for a second or two and said, "Okay, honey. I won't be late."

When everyone was out of the apartment — Joe was downstairs putting Lisa in a cab — Andrew put on an opera recording and then went into the kitchen and turned on the coffeemaker. What a great party! Andrew thought again, but through the joy he knew it would probably be the last party he and Miguel would have.

Joe opened the door partway and called, "Can I come in?"

"Of course!" Andrew called.

"We've got to work on these Q and A's."

"Coffee?" Andrew asked.

"Please."

Andrew went to the kitchen, and while the coffee was brewing, he attached himself to an IV and then poured Joe a cup of coffee and took it out into the living room, pulling his IV stand with his other hand. The coffee was black, and Joe liked sugar and cream, but he said, "Thank you," and accepted it. He had already spread his papers across the table, which was still covered with the red tablecloth from the party. Dozens of votive candles still burned in the window behind the table.

The sight of the IV made Joe very uncomfortable. "Does that hurt?" he asked.

"Sometimes," Andrew said. "Not now." He looked at the IV bag for a second, gauging the flow. "By the way, congratulations, Counselor," he said.

"Congratulations? For what?"

"You survived what I presume to be your first gay party intact." Andrew laughed. "You even danced!"

"You think that's funny?" Joe said. "Let me tell you something, Andrew. When you're brought up like me, like the rest of us in this country, rich, poor, black, white, red, yellow, or green, there's not a whole lot of discussion about homosexuality or 'alternate lifestyles.' You're taught right away as a kid that queers are weird, queers like to dress up in their mother's clothes, queers are afraid to fight, queers are a danger to little kids, all queers want to do is get into your pants. And that still pretty much sums up the general thinking out there, if you want to know the truth."

That was a long speech for Joe to make—he finally had told Andrew exactly how he felt about the whole damned gay thing.

"Thank you for sharing that with me," Andrew said sarcastically.

Joe had had enough of this topic. "Well," he said, "let's get to it. We've got to review these notes for your testimony. Monday's going to be a big day." Joe read a page from the papers on the table. "Okay, I'll ask you to describe the circumstances where you joined the firm of Wyant, Wheeler, Tetlow, Hellerman, and Brown."

Andrew, in the previous few minutes, had begun to think more clearly about death, and life, than he had since his diagnosis; he was not concentrating on Joe's instructions. "Miller?" he said.

"What?"

"Do you pray?"

"That's not the answer to the question, but yes, I pray."

Andrew lost himself in the swelling music for a moment. "What have you prayed for?" he asked.

Joe did not answer at first. He had already broken his rule about no personal relations with clients by coming to the party and even more by bringing his wife. Andrew had even invited his secretary. But then he looked at Andrew, and for the very first time since he had known him he did not think "gay man," he just thought "man who is dying." And if he had been able to articulate it, he would have thought 'friend.' "I prayed for a healthy baby," he said. "I prayed that my wife would make it through the delivery—" He thought for a moment. "I pray for Philadelphia to win the pennant."

"There's a possibility I won't be around for the end of this trial," Andrew said.

"I've considered that," Joe said.

"I've made provisions in my will for some charities, plus Miguel, of course. Miguel will need a lawyer."

"I know a good probate lawyer," Joe said.

"Thanks," Andrew said, "but, Miller?"

"Beckett?"

"I'd appreciate it if you'd help Miguel too, if he needs it."

"Okay," Joe said. He had had enough of this serious talk and wanted to get the conversation back to topics he was comfortable with. "Now, describe the circumstances under which you joined Wyant, Wheeler, Hellerman, Tetlow, and Brown."

Andrew ignored him. "Does this music bother you?" he asked. "Do you even like opera?"

"I'm not all that familiar with opera, Andrew," Joe said. And I hate it, he thought.

"This is my favorite aria coming on now. The soprano is Maria Callas."

Andrew went to the stereo and turned up the volume, filling the room with sound.

"It's from *Andrea Chénier* by Giordano. This is Madeleina singing. She's telling how, during the French Revolution, a mob set fire to her house and her mother died saving her.

"Listen," Andrew said.

" 'I look. The place that cradled me was burning!' " The voice rose with the strings. "Do you hear the heartache in that voice? Do you feel it? Only Callas could sing it like that."

Andrew moved out into the room, pulling his IV pole with him. "Then come the strings, and the music fills with hope. Listen, hear that single cello.

" 'It was during that sorrow that love came to me.

" 'A voice filled with harmony said, Live still! I am life!

" 'Thy heaven is in my eyes!

" 'Thou art not alone!

" 'I gather thy tears,

" 'I walk along thy path and sustain thee.

" 'Smile and hope, for I am love.' "

Andrew stopped translating, just listening, lost in the beauty of the voice, of the music, of the poetry, and then as the aria ended he translated the last line:

" 'I am Love! Love! Love!' "

Oh that poor guy, Joe thought, it just isn't fair. What did he do to deserve this? He's a better lawyer than I'll ever be, and what's he got left, a month? Two?

Andy looked back at Joe. "I'll look at those Q and A's now," he said.

"No," Joe said. He could not think about them himself; all he could think of was how brave Andrew was and how much Andrew loved life and how much knowing Andrew had changed his own life. "You're ready, you're ready." He put his papers in his briefcase. "See you Monday, Beckett," he said, and the warmth in his voice was genuine. "I'll let myself out, so you don't have to drag that thing too far."

As Joe went to the door, Andrew went to the stereo and put the aria on again, even louder, so loud it could be heard outside. Joe stood in the hall and listened for a moment and then turned around and went back to Andrew's door. He wanted to tell Andrew that he was all right for sure in Joe's book and not to worry about it ever again. But the music rose more and more and Joe knew that Andrew would be lost in it, and he did not want to interrupt that mood, so he turned back and called for the elevator.

Inside Andrew danced, he danced for life, he danced

for music, he danced for love, he danced for hope, and as the music expanded and grew he danced more freely, unhooking his IV, and he danced for death. He was not ready, but he was getting there, it was becoming a reality, a visible part of his life, and he started the aria again, singing along in parts; "Live! . . . I am life! . . . I am love!"

Eight

ndrew and Miguel both dressed with care Monday
morning, because that was the day that Andrew was
to begin testifying. After the euphoria from the party
wore off, Andrew was exhausted, and he spent most of that
Sunday in bed, and even then it was very difficult to get up
early on Monday. He had insisted that Miguel not miss any
more classes — "We need somebody working," he had said —
but Miguel argued there was no way they were going to
put his lover on the stand without his being there. Andrew
was too tired to fight back.

They arrived in the courtroom just two minutes before
nine, and promptly at nine Judge Garnett entered. As soon
as everyone was seated again, he began.

"Counsel, call your next witness, please."

"Plaintiff calls Andrew Beckett," Joe said.

This is it, Andrew thought, this is where all of these
months, all of Joe's work, all of my work, all of the anxiety,

have been leading: Either the jury believes me or it does not. Andrew rose and walked slowly to the witness box; everyone in the room could see that he was weak. Even Mr. Wheeler was concerned, although of course he would never show it. Probably the only person unmoved was Mr. Kenton, who was thinking, Good, that faggot's going to get what he deserves.

When Andrew was seated, a bailiff brought him a Bible and said, "Place your left hand on the Bible and raise your right hand. Do you swear to tell the whole truth and nothing but the truth so help you God?"

"I do," Andrew said. The moment he had been dreading, yet the moment they had been working toward all those months was finally here.

Joe eased into the questioning, avoiding the entire issue of AIDS and homosexuality. "Can you describe the circumstances in which you joined the firm Wyant, Wheeler, Hellerman, Tetlow and Brown?"

Andrew spoke quietly and carefully. "Wyant, Wheeler had aggressively recruited me. They were the most prestigious firm in Philadelphia, full of opportunity. And I was impressed by the partners."

"Including Charles Wheeler?"

"Particularly Charles," Andrew said, and it was the truth.

Joe turned to look at Mr. Wheeler and then looked back at Andrew. "What impressed you about him?" he asked.

Andrew thought for a moment. He wanted to answer truthfully, and he wanted to express himself well. "He was the kind of lawyer I thought I wanted to be," Andrew said.

"What kind of lawyer is that?" Joe asked.

Andrew spoke more confidently. "Possessed of an encyclopedic knowledge of the law. A razor-sharp litigator, a genuine leader, gifted at bringing out the very best in others." He paused for a moment to think, then continued. "Charles has an awesome ability to illuminate the most complex legal concepts to colleagues, in the courtroom, even to the person on the street. The kind of person who plays three sets of tennis but doesn't sweat. But underneath the elegant surface, he has an adventurous spirit."

Ms. Conine wrote some notes, and Miguel and Andrew's family all smiled at Andrew, hoping that this would all come out all right. Sarah remembered when Andrew had first been hired by Wyant, Wheeler and how happy he had been and how much he had talked about Charles Wheeler and what a privilege it was to work for him, and she wondered why it made so much difference to Mr. Wheeler that her son was gay and that he had AIDS. What did that have to do with the kind of lawyer he was?

"Obviously, at this time, you weren't sick," Joe said.

"I don't know," Andrew answered. "It's possible I was infected with the HIV virus at that time, but I wasn't diagnosed until several years later."

"You didn't look then the way you look now?" Joe asked.

"No," Andrew said. "I was thirty pounds heavier. I was athletic."

This was something Joe hadn't asked Andrew about, and he thought for a moment before he pursued it.

"How were you athletic?" Joe asked. I hope he doesn't say something like bowling or ballroom dancing, Joe thought.

"I played intramural softball, volleyball, and tennis all through college and law school," Andrew said. "I only stopped playing on teams when I came to Wyant, Wheeler. I could never be sure that I'd be able to show up."

Good, Joe thought. "So you were a regular all-American guy?"

"I suppose you could say that," Andrew answered.

Now the questions had to get tougher, and Joe was surprised to find himself saying a little prayer: "Help Beckett." Not "Help Beckett so we can win," but just "Help Beckett."

"Except that you were gay?" Joe said to Andrew.

"And I still am," Andrew answered. Several spectators laughed, and even Ms. Conine couldn't stop a smile. Matt punched Miguel in the ribs and said, "That's my bro!" The ex-Marine juror frowned.

Joe pushed on. "In the years you worked at Wyant, Wheeler, did you ever tell Charles Wheeler you were gay?"

"No. I did not."

"Can you explain to me *why* you didn't?" Joe asked.

"You don't bring your personal life into a law firm.

You're not supposed to *have* a personal life, really. Anyway, I did plan to tell Charles, eventually. But then this thing happened at the racquet club about three years ago."

"Tell us about it," Joe said.

"Well, we were all in the locker room after a match, and somebody started telling gay jokes." Andrew remembered the scene with disgust: fat, naked, old men sitting in a marble steam room with towels across their laps, all doing their male-bonding thing.

"Do you remember one?" Joe asked.

" 'How does a faggot fake an orgasm?' "

"And the answer was?"

" 'He spits on your back.' "

There were various reactions of amusement or disgust in the courtroom, but surprisingly Ms. Conine did not object. She thought that the joke was disgusting.

"How did Mr. Wheeler react to this?" Joe asked.

"He told the joke," Andrew said, "and some others."

"How did that make you feel?"

"Relieved," Andrew said.

"Relieved?" Joe asked. It was certainly not the answer he had expected.

"Relieved that I'd never told him I was gay. Very relieved."

At that moment Ms. Conine thought that Mr. Wheeler was as disgusting as the joke. She would have been even more unhappy if Andrew had recounted the sexist jokes the partners had told.

"Are you a good lawyer?" Joe asked.

That's what this case is about, Andrew thought. "I am an excellent lawyer," he said.

"What makes you an excellent lawyer?"

"I love the law. I know the law. I excel at practicing it." Andrew stopped to consider whether he should bring up his law school grades but decided against it. "It's the only thing I've ever wanted to do," he said.

"What do you love about it?" Joe asked.

"That's hard to say," Andrew told him. "I love the work itself, the complexity, the puzzles, but I guess what I love the most is that every once in a while, not that often, but occasionally you get to be part of justice being done. It's really a thrill when that happens."

Joe kept Andrew on the stand the entire day, going over detail after detail of his cases, showing how he had consistently won, going over his published articles—there were three—getting Andrew to tell the court about every award he had ever won, and there were many. By the end of the day, Andrew was exhausted, and then when he got home he had to stay hooked up to an IV for almost four hours. Then there were a few hours of ragged sleep and it was time to get up and do it all over again, except that this time the questions would be coming from Ms. Conine, and they would not be friendly. Andrew actually thought about Ms. Conine in the car on the way to court, and he felt some compassion for her situation: What would happen if she lost this case? Wyant, Wheeler would certainly not be pleased, which would mean that the managing partners of her firm would not be pleased either.

By the time they reached the courthouse, Andrew was feeling ill and he immediately headed for the men's room. After he splashed some water on his face he felt a little better and as he turned to leave, Mr. Wheeler came in. It was the first time they had seen each other alone in almost a year.

"Charles!" Andrew said.

"Andy!"

It was an uncomfortable moment, and Mr. Wheeler looked as though he was going to turn around and leave. "Oh please, come in, Charles," Andrew said.

Mr. Wheeler closed the door and they just looked at each other for a moment, and then Mr. Wheeler said, "Andy, I must thank you for your kind and wonderful words in there yesterday."

"They were merely an accurate description of my estimation of your abilities," Andrew said. He was certainly not ready to become friends again, or even friendly.

"I never expected that you and I would find ourselves on opposite sides of any issue," Mr. Wheeler said.

And whose fault is that? Andrew thought. "Nonetheless, here we are."

Mr. Wheeler did not know exactly what to say for probably the first time in his adult life. "Andy, I hope . . . when this is over . . . I wish the best for you. That may sound insincere, it may sound like a pathetic plea for forgiveness, even some kind of last-minute legal maneuver —"

"Or all of the above," Andrew finished.

"—But it happens to be the truth," Mr. Wheeler said.

"Thank you, Charles," Andrew said, and he walked slowly from the room, fatigue showing in his face and in his step.

God, let him live, Mr. Wheeler prayed silently.

It was obvious from the very first question that Ms. Conine, whatever she might think of the case personally, intended to be as rough as possible on Andrew. She did not even ask any warm-up questions but started in with a line of questioning that Joe had hoped she would have the decency to avoid.

"Mr. Beckett, you said yesterday that you aspired to be the kind of person who had 'an adventurous spirit.' Is that correct?"

"Something like that," Andrew answered.

"Do you take risks?"

"In my work?" Andrew asked.

"Any risks?"

"In my work, yes. Calculated risks. You have to."

"You were loyal to Wyant, Wheeler?" Ms. Conine asked.

"I believe I was."

"You worked long hours. You billed many hours a week?" Ms. Conine smiled encouragingly, and Joe thought, What is that snake up to?

"I frequently billed sixty to seventy hours a week," Andrew told her.

"Worked weekends?"

"What's a weekend?" Andrew asked.

"Tell me about it," Ms. Conine said, as though they had something in common, but then she attacked again without taking a breath. "Did your doctor ever tell you to reduce stress? That long hours and stressful working conditions might damage the immune system and speed up the illness?"

"Yes, my doctor mentioned the impact stress can have on the immune system," Andrew admitted.

"So," Ms. Conine said, "in working all those hours, you were ignoring your doctor's orders, being reckless with your own health?"

Andrew did not like the point she was trying to make at all, and neither did his family. Mr. Wheeler, however, was pleased with it. It was an additional line of defense he had not considered, and he rather liked the idea that perhaps they had actually helped Andrew by firing him.

"Are you saying Charles Wheeler fired me for my own good?" Andrew demanded.

"I suggested no such thing." Ms. Conine was pleased that Andrew himself had put the idea into the jurors' minds.

Andrew continued: "I loved being a lawyer. I was an effective lawyer. No one had the right to take that away from me—"

Ms. Conine cut him off before he could say anything

that she might not want the jury to hear. "Have you ever been to the Stallion Showcase Cinema on Twenty-first Street?" she asked.

Uh oh, Joe thought, I hope Andrew can handle this.

"I have been to that theater exactly three times in my life," Andrew said, and he knew where this questioning was going. They must have spent a fortune on private detectives to find something like this out, he thought.

"What kind of movies do they show there?" Ms. Conine asked sweetly.

"Gay movies."

"Gay pornographic movies?" Ms. Conine asked. She was purposely keeping her voice low, her tone low-key.

"Yes," Andrew answered, and once again, in the audience Miguel muttered, "I'm going to get her." Once again, Matt agreed with him.

"Do men have sex with each other in that theater?" Ms. Conine asked.

"Yes, they do." Why wasn't Joe objecting?

"Objection, Your Honor!" Joe said.

Thank God, Andrew thought.

"Your Honor, this line of questioning is pertinent to credibility," Ms. Conine said.

"I'll allow it," Judge Garnett said. "Continue."

"Bastard," Miguel spat, and this time someone at the defense table heard him and turned around to look. Miguel stared back hard.

"Mr. Beckett, have you ever had sex with someone in that theater?"

Andrew did not answer.

"Mr. Beckett, did you ever have sex in that theater?"

"Yes, once."

"When?" Ms. Conine asked. "Approximately what year did this event take place?"

"I guess it was eighty-four or eighty-five," Andrew said.

Good, Ms. Conine thought, he admitted it so we don't have to call that sleazy witness. "Were you aware in nineteen eighty-four or nineteen eighty-five that there was a fatal disease out there called AIDS, and that you could contract it through sexual activity?" she asked.

Andrew wiped his forehead. He was beginning to feel very ill. "It's impossible to know exactly when or how I was infected with HIV," he said. His voice broke a little, from exhaustion, not emotion, and his mother and Miguel sat forward.

Ms. Conine pushed on. "But you were having anonymous sex in porno theaters in nineteen eighty-four or nineteen eighty-five?"

"I told you," Andrew said, "that happened once. People weren't talking about AIDS then the way we are now. Or safe sex."

"But you'd heard of AIDS in nineteen eighty-four or nineteen eighty-five, hadn't you?"

"Yes," Andrew admitted. He was perspiring heavily and was obviously exhausted, and Belinda Conine had never hated the case more than at that moment. "Do you need a break?" she asked.

"No," Andrew said, his voice very weak, "but could I have some water, please?"

By then everyone in the courtroom was concerned about Andrew, including Judge Garnett. "Are you sure you can continue?" the judge asked.

"I'm fine," Andrew said, "but I really would like some water."

The judge asked the bailiff to get Andrew a glass of water, and for a minute or two there was quiet in the room. Everyone, even Charles Wheeler, even Mr. Kenton, wished the trial would come to a speedy end before it totally destroyed what little was left of Andrew's health.

After Andrew took a drink the judge asked him again if he could continue, and when Andrew said he could, Ms. Conine began a new, equally tough line of questioning.

"While you were employed at Wyant, Wheeler, you did everything you could to make sure no one knew you were an active homosexual, correct?"

"That is *not* correct," Andrew said. "I never lied about it."

"Did you keep a picture of your lover on your desk?"

"No."

"Do other lawyers at the firm keep pictures of their spouses or fiancées on their desks?"

"Yes, they do," Andrew said, "but I kept a picture *by* my lover on the wall of my office."

Fine, Ms. Conine thought, he's saying exactly what I want him to. "Mr. Beckett, as a homosexual, one is often forced to conceal one's sexuality, is that right?"

"Some people feel they have to do it in some situations," Andrew answered. His responses were getting slower and weaker.

"Isn't it true you live your life pretending to be something you're not?" Ms. Conine asked. "So much so that the art of concealment and dishonesty has become second nature to you?"

"Objection!" Joe yelled.

"I'll withdraw it," Ms. Conine said; the jury heard that, she thought, and she immediately attacked on another front, aware that she was tearing Andrew down physically as well. "Mr. Beckett? Were you living with Miguel Alvarez in nineteen eighty-four or nineteen eighty-five when you had your anonymous sexual encounter in the porn theater?"

"Yes," Andrew said.

"You could have infected him, isn't that right?" Ms. Conine insisted.

In the audience, Miguel was furious, and Andrew's family was very concerned. They had seen Andrew throughout his illness, but he had always concealed the worst from them, and now, in open court they saw for themselves how weak, how sick, Andrew really was.

"Miguel has not been infected." Thank God, he thought.

Ms. Conine pressed the point. "Mr. Beckett, you

haven't answered my question. You could have infected Mr. Alvarez, isn't that correct?"

"Yes," Andrew said quietly, and I am so sorry, he thought.

Ms. Conine was making every point that she wanted to make, and in exactly the order she wanted, and now it was time to deal with Joe's reasoning that led from Mr. Kenton knowing what KS lesions were to knowing Andrew had AIDS. She began gently.

"You've testified that the lesions on your face were visible to the people you worked with. Is that correct?"

"That's right," Andrew said. "It's in the record."

"And it is your contention that when the partners were made aware of the lesions, they jumped to the conclusion you had AIDS, and fired you. Is that correct?"

Andrew thought about his answer carefully, and then replied, "As painful as it is to accuse my former colleagues of such reprehensible behavior, it's the only conclusion I can come to."

Now for the important part, Ms. Conine thought. "Do you have any lesions on your face at this time?" she asked.

Andrew looked puzzled. "One," he said. "Here, in front of my ear."

"Your Honor, may I approach the witness?" Ms. Conine asked.

Joe was immediately worried. He thought he knew exactly what she was about to do, and the result could be disastrous to his case.

"Is it important?" Judge Garnett asked. Do not harass this witness any more, both his tone and his expression said.

"It is," Ms. Conine said.

"Then you may," Judge Garnett said reluctantly.

Ms. Conine took a hand mirror from a bag on the defense table and held it in front of Andrew. "Remembering that you are under oath, answering truthfully, can you see the lesion on your face, in this mirror, three feet away?"

Andrew tried to concentrate. "Answer truthfully," Ms. Conine warned again.

Andrew spoke with tremendous exhaustion in his voice. "At the time I was fired, there were four lesions on my face, much bigger than —"

"Just answer the question, please!" Ms. Conine insisted.

"No," Andrew said. "I can't really see it."

"No, you cannot," she said to Andrew. She knew the point was not lost on the jury.

"Thank you, Your Honor. No more questions," she said to the judge, and she returned to her table.

"I hate this case," Ms. Conine whispered to Mr. Green, "and I hate it when clients lie to me." Ms. Conine was beginning to think that Joe and Andrew were right.

The judge was becoming more and more concerned about Andrew's condition, and he wanted Andrew to rest, although it was earlier than usual. "This would be a good time to break for the day," he said.

Joe stood up. "Your Honor," he said. "May I have ten minutes for re-direct?"

"Mr. Beckett? Can you go on for ten minutes?" the judge asked.

"Yes, sir," Andrew said weakly.

"Are you sure?" the judge asked.

"I'm sure," Andrew said.

"I'll only need five! Two minutes, tops!" Joe said. He did not want the jury to leave without hearing his contradictions of Ms. Conine's questions.

"You may have five minutes," the judge said.

Joe knew that what he was about to do would be upsetting to everyone, including his client, and he was really beginning to care about his client. He began easily. "Now, Andrew," he said, "I'm a little confused. Is Miguel Alvarez infected with the AIDS virus?"

"No, he is not," Andrew said.

"Andrew, from what we know about the AIDS virus today, would it be fair to say that anyone who had unprotected sex in nineteen eighty-four or eighty-five, or for that matter nineteen eighty-six or nineteen eighty-two, could have the AIDS virus today?"

"That's a fact," Andrew said.

"May I approach the witness?" Joe asked.

"Yes, you may," the judge said. He thought he knew what Joe was going to do, and he wondered if Ms. Conine realized that she had set a trap for herself.

"May I borrow your mirror, Ms. Conine," Joe asked.

"With pleasure," she said. She did not know what was coming, but now the judge was certain he did.

"Andrew," Joe said gently, "do you have any lesions on any part of your body at this time that resemble the lesions that were on your face at the time you were fired?"

"Yes," Andrew said. "On my chest."

Joe just hoped the judge would allow him to proceed. "If it pleases the court, I'd like to ask Mr. Beckett to open his shirt so that everyone here can have an accurate idea of what we're talking about," he said.

Now Ms. Conine realized what she had done. "Objection, Your Honor!" she called. "It would unfairly influence the jury!"

"Your Honor," Joe said, "if Andrew was forced by his illness to use a wheelchair, would the defense ask him to park it outside because it would unfairly influence the jury? We're talking about AIDS, we're talking about lesions—this *case* is about lesions. Let's see what we're talking about here."

"I'll allow it," Judge Garnett said. "Would you unbutton your shirt, Mr. Beckett?"

"All right," Andrew said, and as he loosened his tie and slowly unbuttoned the front buttons of his shirt it was obvious to everyone in the courtroom how weak he was—he could barely manage the buttons—and when he pulled his shirt open and the lesions became visible, some spectators gasped, some jurors had to look away, and his mother began to cry softly against her husband's shoulder.

When Andrew was finished, Joe handed him the mirror and said, "Andrew, can you see the lesions on your chest?"

"Yes."

"Thank you," Joe said. "No more questions."

"I have another question, Your Honor," Ms. Conine said, angry that Joe had outsmarted her.

"Go ahead," the judge said reluctantly.

"That was very effective," Ms. Conine said. "But I must say I'm surprised, Mr. Beckett, after your glowing remarks about justice and the beauty of the law, to see you and your attorney turn this courtroom into a carnival sideshow!"

"I didn't bring the mirror into the courtroom, Ms. Conine, you did!" Joe said.

Ms. Conine still tried to repair some of the damage to her case. "Isn't it true," she said, "that when you went into the office, you covered your lesions with makeup, which you had been taught to apply by a professional makeup artist?"

"The makeup was not effective," Andrew said.

Ms. Conine knew that if she did not quit she could have the jury feeling sorry for Andrew, which would certainly damage her case more than it already had been damaged. "Thank you for your honesty on this point," she said. "No more questions, Your Honor."

"This would definitely be a good time to break for the day," Judge Garnett said, and everyone in the courtroom agreed with him.

It was a hard week for Andrew. He had trouble with his vision, he could not concentrate on what was being said in court, he was terribly weak, he was constantly sick to his stomach. Every day, Joe and Miguel urged him to allow Joe to postpone the trial for a few days so he could get some strength back, but he refused: He would not give up until he saw Charles Wheeler on the stand. Joe had not called him—thinking, correctly, that Mr. Kenton would make the plaintiff's case better—so it was up to the defense. They finally called Mr. Wheeler on Friday. When the bailiff administered the oath Wheeler, dressed in his best suit and a beautiful blue and white striped tie, placed his hand firmly on the Bible and when asked if he swore to tell the truth, he answered in a strong, confident voice, "I do."

Ms. Conine led the questioning after Mr. Wheeler was seated. "Mr. Wheeler, were you aware that Andrew Beckett was suffering from AIDS at the time of his departure from Wyant, Wheeler?"

"No, I was not," Mr. Wheeler said.

"Now for absolute clarity on this point," Ms. Conine said deliberately, looking at the jury then back at Mr. Wheeler, "did you fire Andrew Beckett because he had AIDS?"

"No, I did not fire Andrew Beckett because he had AIDS," Mr. Wheeler said.

Mr. Wheeler was at home in a courtroom and he had convinced more juries than Ms. Conine had ever seen, so her strategy was just to give him general questions and let him talk. The order of the questions was intended to make her case piece by piece. "Mr. Wheeler," she said, "can you explain, in a way that will leave no doubt, why you promoted Andrew Beckett through your firm, and, most importantly, why you eventually asked him to leave?"

Mr. Wheeler settled back in his chair comfortably. "If you're the owner of a major league ball club, you recruit the hot rookie. And Andy was a tremendously promising young attorney. Fresh out of Penn, a crackerjack. That's why we went after him, that's why we hired him, and that's why we stuck with him, year after year."

"Why did you give him opportunity after opportunity?" Ms. Conine asked.

"When you've groomed someone the way we groomed Andy, nurturing him, lavishing all kinds of special treatment on him, you've made quite an investment. We were waiting for his promise to kick in, and deliver. But, ultimately, we could no longer ignore the gap between the promise and reality."

Andrew was stunned to hear Mr. Wheeler saying this. He was actually lying under oath. Andrew tried to concentrate enough to make notes for Joe to use during his cross-examination, but he could not. He could barely think, and disjointed memories of conversations having to do with the case flashed through his mind.

"This is one of the saddest times in my life," Mr. Wheeler went on, with grave importance in his voice. "To sit in this court, testifying to Andy's ultimate failure to make the grade. To discover that he is one of those people who wants to benefit from the system, but doesn't want to play by the system's rules. To think you know someone, only to find out you don't know them at all. It's heartbreaking."

"Thank you. That's all for now, Your Honor," Ms. Conine said.

"Mr. Miller?" Judge Garnett said.

Joe knew he had to do something to break through Mr. Wheeler's smooth facade, to rattle him, so he started by clapping his hands. "Mr. Wheeler, you're magnificent! Andrew was right! You're a great lawyer! Are you gay?"

"How *dare* you!" Mr. Wheeler said.

"Objection!" Ms. Conine yelled.

Joe rushed on before the judge had time to rule. "How dare I what, sir? Ask you a simple question about your sexual orientation? Why does this question disturb you so?"

Andrew shook his head but he could not concentrate on what was happening in the room. *—I didn't mind covering for Andy, but I did wonder when he was planning to deal with his problem* . . . he heard Rachel say.

"Objection!!" Ms. Conine yelled again.

—If you want to be a leader in this society, you have to make certain sacrifices— Andrew was close to collapse.

"Your Honor," Joe said, "defense has been allowed to explore the most intimate, personal details of my client's life.

Am I not going to be allowed one simple, relevant question?"

"It's a fair question, Ms. Conine," the judge said. "The witness will kindly answer."

"No, I am not a homosexual," Mr. Wheeler said indignantly.

— *You have to make a decision, is this guy partner material?* The voices in Andrew's head were getting stronger.

"But it ruffled your feathers when I asked, didn't it?" Joe said.

"Objection," Ms. Conine said.

"Sustained," the judge ordered.

— *What's that on your forehead, Pal?* Andrew could no longer hold his head up and he held it with his hands with his elbows resting on his knees.

Joe decided to let the objection pass and press on. "Mr. Wheeler, isn't it true that when you realized Andrew Beckett, your golden boy, your future senior partner, was gay, and had AIDS, that drove a stake of fear through your heterosexual heart?"

"Objection!" Ms. Conine said.

Again Joe did not give the judge a chance to rule. "Remembering all the handshakes and the hugs, the intimate moments in the sauna, friendly pats on the backside that you and Andy exchanged like guys do sometimes, didn't you think, My God, what does this say about me?"

— *If you force this case to go to trial you will regret it for the rest of your natural born days.* Andrew's vision began to blur.

"Objection, Your Honor!" Ms. Conine shouted.

"Ms. Conine," Judge Garnett said, "I find this line of questioning appropriate under the circumstances. Will the witness please respond to the question?"

—A trial takes time, Andy, you know what I mean?

Mr. Wheeler was insulted. "Mr. Miller," he said derisively, "you may tap-dance around me all you wish with your innuendos and locker-room fantasies, but the truth remains that your client worked when he wanted to work, telling us what he thought we needed to know about who he really was. Andy insisted on bending the rules. And his work suffered tremendously in the long run as a result of that."

—You could do nothing that would not make us incredibly proud. Andrew could no longer hear the questioning.

Keep talking, and you'll kill your own case, Joe thought. "Explain this to me like I'm a six-year-old," he said. "Who makes the rules, you?"

"Read your Bible, Mr. Miller—the Old and New Testament. You'll find some pretty valuable rules in there," Mr. Wheeler said. He was well satisfied with his answer.

"Mr. Wheeler—"

—What's that on your forehead, Pal?

"Excuse me!" Andrew called, and he tried to stand but his vision faded to gray and then black and he fell unconscious on the floor. People rose to see what had happened,

Miguel yelled, "No!" and leapt over rows of chairs to get to him, Andrew's father held his mother, Andrew's sister rushed forward, "Oh no," Joe said, "please God not now," and Mr. Wheeler yelled, trying to take charge, "Somebody get a doctor! Now!"

This time there was no wait at the emergency room. At the moment the ambulance arrived Dr. Gillman, who had just been leaving the hospital when the call came, was waiting, and Andrew was rushed into a treatment room within a minute. Andrew was gasping hard for breath that did not come, and the first procedure was to put a tube in his lungs for the ventilator, but they encountered difficulty inserting it and the procedure made his breathing worse. Andrew's eyes were round with fear.

"Leave him alone!" Miguel screamed. "You're making it worse! Take it out!"

"Miguel, get out of here," Dr. Gillman said.

"No!" Miguel screamed again, "leave him alone!"

At a signal from Dr. Gillman, a nurse firmly led Miguel out. "I promise you," she said, "I will not let them hurt your friend."

"His name's Andrew!" Miguel yelled.

"I will not let them hurt Andrew," the nurse said, and she led Miguel to an uncomfortable waiting room with cigarette-scarred furniture and tattered magazines. It was more than an hour before Miguel was allowed back in. Andrew looked worse than Miguel, or anyone else, had ever seen him look. The only thing Miguel and Andrew's family had to be happy about that night, and it was a very small thing, was that Dr. Gillman decided not to put Andrew in an intensive care unit but instead found him a private room.

———

The trial continued the next Monday without Andrew there. He was ill, seriously ill, but he was comfortable, just on regular oxygen, not on a ventilator. Andrew's parents spent the day at the hospital, and Miguel wanted to stay with them, but Andrew insisted that he go to court, because, as Andrew said, the case was sure to go to the jury soon, and he wanted Miguel to see the verdict.

Robert Seidman was Ms. Conine's last witness, and when it was Joe's turn to question him he was surprisingly cooperative.

"Did you notice any changes whatsoever in Andrew Beckett's appearance over the course of the year leading up to his termination?" Joe asked.

"Yes, I did," Mr. Seidman said, aware that he was about to anger his partners Mr. Wheeler and Mr. Kenton, at the very least.

"Were the changes for the better or for the worse?" Joe asked.

"Well," Mr. Seidman said, "sometimes they were for the better, but generally they were for the worse."

"Mr. Seidman? What did you think caused these changes in Andrew Beckett's appearance?"

"I was afraid, I suspected, that Andy had AIDS," Mr. Seidman said very quietly, and he had been right; Mr. Wheeler was furious.

"Thank you," Joe said.

"I'd like a few minutes for redirect," Ms. Conine said.

"Mr. Seidman?" she asked. "Did you share your suspicions with Mr. Wheeler and the other managing partners at any time before the decision to fire Andrew Beckett was made?"

"No, I didn't mention it to anyone," Mr. Seidman said. "Not even Andy. I didn't give him a chance to talk about it. And I think I'm going to regret that for the rest of my life."

Nine

*B*eckett v. *Wyant, Wheeler, Hellerman, Tetlow, and Brown*
did not reach the jury for almost another two
weeks, and those final days of the trial were exhausting for everyone. Ms. Conine moved for a mistrial
because Andrew's collapse in the courtroom might have
unfairly influenced the jury, and also because she knew
he would not be around for a retrial if her motion was
granted. Her motion was not granted, but Judge Garnett
did accept several pages of strong language she had written to be included in his instructions to the jury; the essence of the statement was that the jury could not
consider Andrew's current condition in reaching a verdict.

The closing summations took two full days. Joe stuck
to his original strategy — basically the one outlined by Andrew the day after he was fired — to support his assertion
that Andrew had always been an excellent lawyer. He went

over every case that Andrew had handled at Wyant, Wheeler in the six years he was an associate there, beginning with his first motion in the little letter of credit case.

Ms. Conine, being the defense counsel, had the next to the last words, and there were a lot of them, but she tried to make three basic points: Andrew was a mediocre lawyer at best, Andrew tried to impose his lifestyle on the firm — Mr. Wheeler insisted on this point, though Ms. Conine thought it was weak because he never told any of the partners he was gay — and that none of the partners had known Andrew had AIDS.

The final words to the jury were Judge Garnett's. He spent an entire morning instructing the jurors on all of the points of law that were relevant, and he admonished them again and again that their decision must be based only on those points. "Personal prejudices," the judge said, "have no place in the courtroom."

The first vote of the jurors, as soon as they began deliberations, did not go well for Andrew: nine against and three for. Then the arguing began. People can become very emotional about homosexuality, and these jurors were. Fortunately, the ex-Marine foreman had been a drill sergeant, and he kept everyone more or less in line without ever giving his own opinions.

The jurors were sick of this case too, and tempers were short on the morning of the second full day of deliberations.

"Why didn't he tell them he had AIDS? Was he going to wait until he had infected everyone else?"

"He didn't care about the people he worked with, or he would have let them know they were working with an AIDS person!"

"Yes! These people have an *obligation* to tell others about their situation so we can decide if we want to take a chance working with them, going to school with them, or whatever."

There was an occasional voice of reason.

"You can't get AIDS like that!"

"How do you know you can't? It's never been proved to me. Maybe you can get it from a mosquito."

"A mosquito!?"

"How would you like to be bitten by a mosquito that had just bitten some homo with AIDS?"

"I don't like Joe Miller's tactics. And Andrew was promiscuous. He was actually having sex in porno theaters when he already had a 'lover,' as they call it."

"What else would you call it?"

"That is not the issue here!"

This went on for the entire morning, with nothing being decided, and after a break for lunch the afternoon started out the same way, although Andrew's supporters were more vocal.

"They were so mean to that young man? I can't believe what they put him through."

"I don't trust all those men in their fancy suits. If you ask me, Andrew *was* a good lawyer!"

The foreman was actually very wise. He knew that they could not reach a decision until everyone had had a chance to express everything they wanted to about homosexuals, AIDS, and probably, given the emotions in this case, motherhood and the Catholic Church as well, so he just sat and listened, occasionally calming someone down or bringing him or her back to somewhere near the topic if they strayed too far. Finally, the other jurors began to notice what he was doing and then they began to resent it.

"You're the foreman and you haven't said anything. What do you think?"

"Yeah, let's hear your opinion."

"You can't just sit there!"

"Boy, he'll fix that homo," one juror said to another quietly.

The foreman waited until everyone was still, no one was talking, everyone was listening, watching.

"They're saying he wasn't a good lawyer," he said quietly. "He was mediocre. And even though they gave him the most important case they'd ever had, for one of their most important clients, they claim that doesn't prove anything because it was just a test. What did they call it? 'A carrot'—"

"Hey, what's up, doc," one of the jurors interjected, and then was immediately quiet when anger flashed across the foreman's face for just a second.

"They said they wanted to see if he'd rise to the occasion," the Marine continued. "Okay, say I've got to send a pilot into enemy territory, and he's going to be flying a plane that costs three hundred fifty million dollars. Who am I going to put into that plane? A rookie pilot who can't cut the grade, just because I want to see if he'll rise to the challenge? Or am I going to give the assignment to my best pilot, my most experienced, my sharpest? I just don't get it."

At four o'clock that afternoon they sent a message to the judge that they were ready, and the courtroom was packed when they came back in; only Miguel and most of Andrew's family were absent, because they were at the hospital.

Judge Garnett was very glad that this trial was ending, and although he had never admitted it to anyone, not even his wife, he hoped that Andrew won. "Members of the jury, have you reached a verdict?"

"We have, Your Honor," the foreman said.

Joe tried to read the verdict from the jurors' faces. It did not look good because the ex-Marine looked pleased. The defense team saw the juror's expression as well, and they were very confident.

"Do the majority agree?"

"Yes, Your Honor."

"Would you please state your verdict."

This is it, Joe thought, I've just wasted six months of my life.

"We find for the plaintiff, Andrew Beckett."

There was a murmur of conversation through the courtroom, and there was a whispered conference at the defense table. "Your Honor, may the jury be polled?" Ms. Conine asked.

"Yes. Bailiff, poll the jury," the judge directed.

The poll showed ten for and two against. It was over, almost.

"Have you awarded any damages?" the judge asked.

"Yes, we have, Your Honor."

The managing partners of Wyant, Wheeler were very tense.

"For back pay and loss of benefits, one hundred forty-three thousand dollars."

Mr. Wheeler smiled; that was nothing. Joe was disappointed; it was better than no win at all, but not much better.

"For damages related to mental anguish and humiliation we award two hundred and fifty thousand dollars."

Easy—almost as good as winning, Mr. Wheeler thought, and Joe would have agreed with him.

"And for punitive damages, we award four million seven hundred and thirty-two thousand dollars."

"Yes!" Joe shouted. "Yes!" he yelled, throwing his pencil into the air. There was an explosion of shouts from the spectators. Andrew's brother Matt was on his feet and at the plaintiff's table in seconds, shaking Joe's hand.

Andrew was doing very poorly, and Dr. Gillman was performing a part of her job that no amount of training or experience could ever make easier: telling Andrew's parents and Miguel as gently as possible that Andrew was not going to get better, telling them that Andrew was dying. "If he comes out of the hospital this time, which is unlikely, you mustn't expect him to be remotely like he was before this crisis. He's lost the vision in his right eye because of the CMV and he won't get it back. And the CMV has also ravaged his lungs."

Joe passed just then and heard the end of what the doctor was saying, and as happy as he was, he found himself saying, God, don't take him now, please, and he quickened his step.

Andrew was almost unrecognizable; most of his hair was gone, his face and his arms were very very thin, his complexion was gray, and an oxygen mask covered his face. Matt was already there, telling Andrew and the siblings about the end of the trial, and they applauded when Joe came in. Andrew smiled weakly, and he motioned with his hand for Joe to come closer and Andrew's family went outside. He wanted to be alone with Joe, the attorney he had once looked down on, the man he had come to respect and care for, the man who had come to care for him.

"I brought champagne. Dom Perignon!" Joe said.

Andy patted the bed beside him, and Joe put the bottle on the bed table and sat next to Andrew.

"How're you doing?" Joe asked. He could not believe how much he cared for this man, the man who had taught him more about prejudice than he had learned before in his lifetime, the man who had taught him so much about the law, the man who had taught him so much about life.

Andrew was so weak he could barely take off his oxygen mask. "What do you call a thousand lawyers chained to the bottom of the ocean?" he asked, ignoring Joe's question.

"I don't know," Joe said.

"A good start," Andrew told him, trying to smile and then he was serious. "Excellent work, Counselor. I thank you." He patted Joe's hand and Joe put his other hand on top of Andrew's and held it, and as he did, he remembered the time he was upset even shaking Andrew's hand. You son of a bitch, he thought, you have really made me care about you.

"It was great working with you, Andrew," Joe said. He felt his voice crack with emotion. "You're very welcome."

Andrew was having trouble breathing, and he pulled his hand away and tried to put his mask back over his face. But Joe gently took Andrew's hands away and gently positioned the mask himself.

"I'd better go," Joe said then. There was so much he wanted to say that he couldn't say.

"Sure thing," Andrew said.

"I'll see you later," Joe said.

Andrew paused. "Thanks for stopping by."

"I *will* see you later," Joe repeated, hoping that he would.

"Congratulations again," Andrew said.

Sarah came in as Joe was leaving, and she gave him a hug and said, "I just want to thank you, you were terrific."

"And so are you," Joe said.

As he left, one by one the family came in and said a few words to Andrew.

"I'll see you tomorrow, okay?" Matt said, and Andrew did not answer. "Okay?" Matt said again, and Andrew just smiled. Andrew thought that this was probably the important good-bye, the final good-bye, but he did not want anyone to know that.

"Good night, Son," his father said. "Try to get some rest." Andrew squeezed his hand, and his father said, "I love you, Andy." His father knew what Andrew knew, and he did not say that he would see Andrew tomorrow.

"I love you too, Dad," Andrew said softly.

Randy started to speak but could not get the words out. Suddenly he laid his head on Andrew's chest and sobbed, "Oh God, Andy!"

"Hey, I'll see you tomorrow," Andrew said weakly.

Sarah put her arm around Randy and helped him walk

out of the room. The rest of the family followed, each of them embracing Miguel as they left. "Andy's very lucky to have you," Andrew's father said, and then he closed the door and Miguel and Andrew were alone.

Miguel held Andrew and kissed him and then they did not speak but remembered together, remembered times of happiness, of sailing, of doing the simple day-to-day tasks of life together. They remembered the time they got the wedding rings they wore, and through the remembering Andrew worried about what Miguel would do without him but there was nothing he could do about it, his fight was over, his time was over, all there was left to do was leave. Andrew reached up and tried to take off the mask and Miguel had to help him and when it was off Andrew said, "Miguel, I'm ready." Miguel would not lose control, not now, not yet, there would be time for that later, and then, although they both knew that Andrew was almost gone, Miguel said, "Are you ready for *Wheel of Fortune*?" and he turned on the television and lay on the bed beside Andrew and put on Andrew's mask. He held Andrew's hand and then lay back on the pillow beside his lover and closed his eyes and listened to Andrew breathe and as the show went on, Andrew closed his eyes also and he drifted into sleep. Over the next few hours his breathing slowed and became quieter and quieter and Miguel turned off the television and held Andrew gently and stroked his head and as Andrew's breathing slowed even more, Miguel whispered, "I love you, Drew," and he pushed aside the oxygen tube and gently kissed Andrew's lips and held him as his temperature dropped and his heartbeat grew even slower, and his face became tranquil, almost like a child's.

Miguel called their apartment first, where Andrew's mother and father were staying, and Andrew's parents were calm, concerned about Miguel, knowing, accepting, glad for Andrew that it was over and he was suffering no more; their grief would come later.

The phone rang in Joe and Lisa's bedroom a little after midnight, but Joe slept through its ringing. Finally Lisa answered. She listened for a minute and had nothing to say. By then Joe was awake, and she handed him the phone and said, "It's Miguel." Joe listened and said almost nothing and when he hung up, he turned his head into his pillow and sobbed; he could not be comforted.

Andrew Beckett was a happy baby, always smiling, laughing. When he was very small he would lay in his crib on his back and try to pull his foot into his mouth, smiling as he did it. If someone talked to him or touched him he would shake his arms and legs in the air and give the world a smile of beautiful innocence that defies accurate description; only someone who has seen such a baby could truly understand.

Andrew was his parents' first, and they were free with expressions like "miracle" and "a gift from God." Like all new parents, they wanted to share their joy, and from the time they brought Andrew home from the hospital, sleeping like an angel in his mother's arms, their house was filled with family and friends. Aunts, uncles, cousins, neighbors, people who worked with Andrew's father were all invited in to see the new baby, and everyone agreed that rarely was such a good baby, such a beautiful baby, to be found.

And his parents were so proud. "He's going to grow into a big, strong boy," his father said when Andrew showed some of his future precociousness by crawling at the unusually young age of four months. He demonstrated his physical abilities and caused an immediate child-proofing of the house in an incident that was much more alarming to his parents than to young Andrew. They had left him safely on a blanket in the middle of the living room rug while his father went to the kitchen to help his mother reach an overhead cabinet. They did not leave Andrew alone for more than a minute or two, but it was long enough for him to crawl to the edge of the rug, grab the fringe of a cloth that covered a marble-topped table, and pull the cloth, plus the lamp and knickknacks on the table, crashing to the floor. Andrew gave a cry of surprise, and the noise and Andrew's cry brought his parents running from the kitchen, his mother screaming. It was not necessary; Andrew was sitting in the middle of the mess smiling. "Yeup," his father said proudly, "we're going to have a big, strong boy on our hands. He's really going to be something someday."

CHRISTOPHER DAVIS is the author of the novels *Joseph and the Old Man* and *Valley of the Shadow*, and a story collection, *The Boys in the Bars*. He lives in Manhattan.

RON NYSWANER wrote the screenplays for *Smithereens*, *Mrs. Soffel*, and *Love Hurts*, co-authored *Gross Anatomy*, and wrote and directed *The Prince of Pennsylvania*. Currently, he is working on a script about schizophrenia for Jodie Foster; adapting Edith Wharton's *The Glimpses of the Moon* for Lawrence Kasdan; and planning a project about religious faith in America for Jonathan Demme.

DON'T MISS
THESE CURRENT
BANTAM BESTSELLERS